ECHOES OF A

On a sunny afternoon in Selbc
gate and gazed out across a gre
eye the grass changed in shap
field of golden corn; and standing at its edge was a boy.

He had light brown hair and friendly grey eyes; and when he smiled at me, I knew it was James ...

... and this is his story.

About the Author:

Jean Newland was born in Four Marks and has lived all her life in Hampshire. Since discovering her close family connection with the legendary 'Trumpeter' she has researched the family from the early days in Selborne to the years spent in Bentley, where her father was born in 1901.

ECHOES OF A TRUMPET

Jean Newland

Echoes of a Trumpet
First published 1998

Typeset and published by John Owen Smith
12 Hillside Close, Headley Down, Hampshire GU35 8BL
Tel/Fax: 01428 712892
E-mail: wordsmith@headley1.demon.co.uk

ISBN 1-873855-30-3

Cover printed by Pier House Ltd, Bourne Mill, Farnham, Surrey

Text printed and bound by Antony Rowe Ltd, Bumper's Farm,
Chippenham, Wiltshire

THANK YOU!

To Ted for his patience, and the many cups of tea;

To my friends at Phœnix Writers Circle for their encouragement;

To Jo Smith, for his support and help with research into the Riots which was invaluable in the completion of this book;

And a special mention for Mary Clark (she knows why).

Descendants of John Newland

JOHN NEWLAND m. **Ann** EVANS

Frederick · John · Jane · Ellen · Arthur · William · **JAMES** · Eliza · Harriet

Ellen
m.
Robert
HEATH

JAMES
m.
Mary Ann
KNIGHT

Mary

FREDERICK
m.
Caroline
COLES

James · **FREDERICK** · George · Thomas

Frederick · Florence · James · Joseph · Owen · Thomas · Rosalie · Eva · **ARTHUR** · Robert · Percy

ARTHUR
m.
Dorothy Laura
TRIBE

JEAN · Beryl

Chapter One

"Where 'as that boy got to?" Ann Newland muttered to herself.

Turning to one of her other children, she asked, "William, go an' see if James is anywhere in sight, will yer?"

The boy scowled behind his mother's back and shifted his bulk reluctantly from behind the kitchen table.

"Can't see 'im," he said, after barely a glance outside. Then re-seating himself, he resumed the rapid consumption of thin gruel, scraping the tin bowl so hard that his mother, fearing for her senses, shouted at him to stop.

Two little girls played happily at the other end of the table.

The woman sighed. If only her youngest son could be so content.

Birdsong filled the early morning air as the boy sat astride the five-bar gate. He gazed spellbound as rabbits, noses twitching, hopped in and out of deep burrows and tiny, scurrying mice sought shelter along the hedgerow.

At the far end of the field a tawny-coated fox moved, body low and nose to the ground, before disappearing through a gap in the hedge.

To ten-year-old James Newland it was the perfect place to be at this time of day, when the world was waking and everything was bright and fresh with dew. The early mist swirled and eddied, melting before his eyes.

The sun was rising steadily in the pale pearlescent sky. Unmarred by clouds, it boded well for another warm and sunny autumn day.

He sighed and shifted his position slightly, slowly drawing one leg over the top of the gate to join the other. Even favourite seats could get just a little uncomfortable when sat on too long. James suddenly realised that he had been here for a long time; perhaps he had better be getting on with his chore and hurry back home. Not that he wanted to go yet, because although his father and older brother Arthur would by now have left for work, the other children would be up and about, filling the small kitchen with bustle and noise.

Reluctantly, he slid down from the gate. Being careful not to make any sudden movement or sound which could frighten the animals he set off across the fields, leaving in his wake a trail of

7

footprints in the dewy grass. Footprints which were surprisingly large for such a small boy, but his boots like the rest of what he wore, had been passed down through the family and had been the only pair available.

Over in the next field he could see what he had come for—mushrooms. He had the task of picking some at least twice a week at this time of year, as they were a welcome supplement to the family's food supply.

Life was hard, not just for his family, but for everyone living in the small Hampshire village of Selborne. It was twelve years since the 'Swing' riots, but work was still scarce in rural areas; the revolt had solved nothing and now many farms had machinery to do the heavier work. James' father had been lucky, being kept on as a labourer at Home Farm when so many had been laid off, and because he had worked for the same man for many years, he felt more secure than some.

Things had become a little easier as the older children left home to work, the boys on farms, the girls mainly in service. Now there were only five out of the original eleven left living in the cramped, thatched cottage on the edge of the village. Arthur, fourteen, worked as a labourer with his father and so earned a shilling, but this still left William, twelve, James, Eliza who was eight and four-year-old Harriet to be fed and clothed.

James' father, John, grew a few vegetables and kept three scruffy hens who supplied an egg or two most days, making them better off than some families who did not have the inclination to do the same.

Occasionally the farm manager would give them a piece of fatty bacon left over from the slaughter and this was greeted with much relish; served with home-made bread and a few fresh vegetables, it was a feast indeed.

Now the sun climbed higher in the sky and James could feel its warmth begin to flow through his slender frame, hidden under the over-large, but clean, shirt and breeches.

He loved the village and surrounding countryside, and childlike, was certain that he would never go and live anywhere else.

He reached the stream which ran merrily along the edge of the field, tinkling its way over stones and the roots of nearby trees. A sprinkling of fallen leaves swirled along the surface, dodging this way and that as the water raced on its way.

James drew in his breath sharply and looked longingly at the stream. It would be so nice to paddle, to feel the cold water between his toes and lapping against his legs. But dare he? There wasn't really time. Then, without another thought, he pulled off his boots and waded in.

Several blissful moments later, after treading his way over the stones and splashing his feet at passing flotsam, the cold penetrated through to his bones and he jumped back onto the grassy bank, pushing his still-wet feet into his boots.

He very soon realised that this had not been a good idea, as the rags in the toes of his boots rapidly became soggy, making walking in the already over-large footwear very difficult. He clomped over to where the mushrooms grew and hastily picked as many as he could find, placing them carefully into the front of his shirt.

It was not too far to go home, but his problem was, what could he wear to school? His mother would be cross when she saw the state of him. His parents were very strict about taking care of things. Having so little in life, it was looked upon with stern disapproval if you spoilt what you did have.

Once in the lane he paused to get his bearings. He just had to check on the blackbird's nest in the hedge. There had been two eggs in it the day before yesterday and he was curious to see if there were any more.

He approached the nest-site cautiously. By standing, with difficulty, on tiptoe he could just see into the tiny, grass and feather lined cup and was rewarded with the sight of four pale-blue, speckled eggs. Then he backed away in the same careful manner. He would have to make sure that no one saw him near, giving the location away. Some of the other boys, his own brother William included, would think nothing of taking the eggs, smashing them and wrecking the nest.

He got upset when this happened, and had on several occasions been made a laughing stock when he tried to stop them. Often the following weeks had been made torture for him, with the boys all punching him and jeering unkindly, calling him soft-in-the-head. But only when there were no adults around.

James found life baffling. For him it was second nature to love all birds and animals, admire the flowers and trees, and he could not understand why others did not feel the same. It made him an outcast and that in turn brought loneliness. There seemed to be no one with whom he could share the wonders which he saw around him every day, no one to tell of the bird's nest or to share in the delight of watching the sun rise over the low hills to the east, or of its fiery decent behind the hanger to the west.

He sighed and carried on his way up the narrow lane. Soon he came to Honeysuckle Cottage, the home of their near neighbours, an elderly couple called Butler.

Mr Butler was leaning on his gate, puffing on a blackened pipe.

"'Allo there, young man, you be out an' about early t'day. Bin out to see if all's well with the world 'ave yer?" the old man asked, a wide smile crossing his broad, florid face. It was well known around the village about the boy's early morning outings.

James swallowed hard. "Mornin', Mr Butler. Yeh, it's a lovely day, ain't it?"

"It certainly is," the man replied. "Goin' to be quite warm later on, shouldn't wonder. Won't yer ma be wonderin' where yer are? Time's gettin' on." He took out his pocket watch and peered at it.

At that moment his wife emerged from the front porch and waddled down the short pathway with its border of pretty flower-beds.

"Ah, it's young James, 'ow are you t'day?" Her jolly face and twinkling blue eyes made the boy smile back, his shyness fading.

"Mornin' Mrs Butler," the boy whispered. "I'm a'right, thanks." Then he asked Mr Butler, "Do yer need any errands t'day?"

"Bless yer lad, I do at that. Could yer ask Mr Bicknell to add an 'alf ounce of me usual baccy to our order, as yer go past the shop. That would be grand, it'll save me poor legs, that's for sure."

James cleared his throat. "I could fetch it for yer," he said, adding slowly, "if yer like."

"Well, well, what a grand little chap yer are and no mistake. What do yer think of that mother?" this last to his wife. He turned once more to the boy. "No, it's a'right thanks lad, you'll make yerself later than ever and we can't 'ave yer missin' yer schoolin', can we?"

Mrs Butler flapped her apron at him, "No, we can't an' yer'd best get on 'ome, yer ma'll be worryin'."

"Bye then. I'll give Mr Bicknell yer message." James continued painfully on his way up the lane.

The couple watched as he went. "It's a shame there aren't a few more like 'im around," said Mrs Butler, "some of the lads hereabouts are nothin' but trouble."

"Aye, that's true. And the youngster gets made fun of an' all. Still I think 'e copes a'right." He smiled fondly at his wife. "We'd best get on—our Charlotte will be 'ere afore we knows it, with little Mary Ann in tow. I bet she's grown since we last saw 'er."

Meanwhile, as James trudged on he thought about the old couple. They were nice people who did a lot to help other folk; he knew this because he had heard his father say. But he liked them mainly because they did not laugh at him like other people did; and he was allowed to help Mr Butler in his garden sometimes after school, being rewarded with a glass of Mrs Butler's homemade ginger beer and the pick of a sweet from the pretty glass jar on the kitchen windowsill. They also gave apples, plums and pears from their garden to his mother so that she could make a pie or some jam. Always a treat to be looked forward to.

At last he arrived home, out of breath and very uncomfortable. He walked slowly into the kitchen and placed the mushrooms carefully on the draining board, trying not to draw attention to himself, or his plight.

"Ah, there yer are at last, I thought yer'd got lost," was all his mother said, then turned her attention back to the big, black pot suspended over the open fire in the grate.

Good, thought James, I don't think she noticed anything. He saw his brother looking at him curiously from his seat at the well-scrubbed table, but ignored him. He would be only too pleased to cause trouble, if he could.

William sniffed, "Where yer bin then, watchin' the birdies?" He sniggered at this and dug Eliza, who was sitting next to him, in the ribs with his elbow, hoping that she would join in the ragging, but their mother broke in sternly.

"That'll do. Come on, get yerselves off to school. James, yer'd better 'ave a slice o' bread, seein' as yer weren't 'ere fer nothin' earlier."

"Thanks, ma." James' candid grey eyes tried not to meet hers. He wondered how he was going to change the rags in his boots—there didn't seem to be any way to do it now.

Then disaster struck.

He turned too quickly and somehow, maybe because of the loose boots, fell over his own feet, landing on the flagstones with a crash. To his horror, the twine on his left boot snapped and his foot shot out into view. On his heel was a huge, bleeding sore where the leather had rubbed his damp skin. For a second James stared at it, not sure what to do. He groaned inwardly—that had given the game away. He scrambled up from the floor and stood in front of his mother fearing the worst.

She tut-tutted. "Oh, son, what 'ave yer done? Look at yer foot. Sit down, let me see t'other one an' all."

He untied the other boot and eased it off. His right foot was red and beginning to blister, but nowhere as bad as the other.

His mother sighed, "I'll get somethin' t' put on 'em," and hurried into the bedroom, returning a few seconds later with two pieces of clean cloth in her hands. These she wrapped carefully around his feet, tucking in the ends and making sure that the sores were well covered. Then she removed the damp rags from inside his boots. "There, that'll 'ave t' do."

James could hardly believe his ears. Was that all she was going to say?

He pulled his boots on. They were still a bit damp but he would just have to put up with it. The walk to school was not something to be looked forward to.

As the children were leaving the cottage, their mother called after them, "Now don't dawdle or yer'll be late. No stoppin' off on the way and straight 'ome t'night as well 'cos yer father needs some 'elp in the garden. James, 'ere's yer bread. Now, do yer 'ear me, no day-dreamin' an' wanderin' off."

This was not said too unkindly, but he felt guilty sometimes about what folk called his 'daydreaming'. He did not mean to be caught up in his surroundings so often, but once something took his attention, he would lose all track of time.

"No, ma, I'll try not to." He took the proffered slice of bread.

His mother smiled, "That's alright then, good boy. 'Urry up now." She watched her children go with a wistful gaze. How different those two boys were. William, so strong, boisterous and, truth be told, a bit of a handful. And, James, just the opposite. She and her husband worried about him. He was far too shy and sensitive, yet old beyond his years; but such a loving, caring child, they would not really have him any other way.

On the journey to school, with his brother jostling him, James began to reflect on the funny way that grown-ups behaved. When you expected to get into trouble you didn't, and yet other times you were scolded, or even worse, and never knew what you were supposed to have done. Then William broke into his thoughts with a playful punch and they chased off down the road, leaving poor Eliza to run behind.

Just in time, James remembered to dash into Mr Bicknell's shop and give him the message from Mr Butler.

When they arrived home from school that afternoon, the first thing the children noticed was the wide smile on their mother's face. This was unusual as the poor woman was normally so busy and harassed that all they got was a brief nod and a quick "'Allo," and "get yer 'ands washed," as they came through the door.

Mrs Newland often took in washing from some of the large houses around the village, just to bring in a few extra pennies. It was hard, back-breaking work for very little reward and on wet days the children would arrive home to a damp and gloomy kitchen, hung around with wet sheets.

Today though, it was cheerful and uncluttered. Harriet was playing happily with her rag doll at the table and the tabby cat lay curled up cosily beside the hearth.

And their mother smiling.

"Ah there yer are, come and sit down, I've somethin' to tell yer."

They scrambled onto the wooden benches which ran one either side of the table. James wondered what could have happened. It must be something good to make ma smile so.

He held his breath in anticipation.

"Now then, it's good news. Yer father's bin given the job of stockman up at the farm. Old Bill Knowles 'as 'ad t' give up 'an Mr Turner 'as decided to give 'is place to yer father. Now it might not seem like much to you, 'im bein' a stockman instead of labourin' but it'll mean nearly double the wage comin' in each week. What's more, they've offered yer father's place to our Arthur, so 'e'll be earnin' more an' all."

The children looked at her in silence for a moment or two. Harriet still played unconcernedly with her doll and Eliza also was too young to know what all the fuss was about.

But James understood. It would mean less patching and mending, less making do with old, worn-out clothes and boots. Perhaps mother could even stop taking in that horrible washing. But best of all, it could mean that when Christmas came around there would be small presents this year. Not that he minded only having homemade wooden things, but he had once seen a boy at school with a compass and had wanted one ever since.

A wide grin spread over his grubby face, "I'm ever so glad for yer ma, an' it's nice to see yer smilin'…"

He stopped and clamped his hand over his mouth, suddenly realising what he had said. He gazed at his mother, eyes wide.

She looked at him quietly for a moment, then said softly. "Oh dear, I'm sorry, I 'adn't realised 'ow glum I'd become. I'll try to smile more often—after all, life should be a little easier for us now."

Mrs Newland reached out to ruffle her son's light-brown hair with her hand. Bless the boy. She could see that he really was pleased at the news, and even William was happily clapping his hands, thoughts of more food on the table no doubt uppermost in his mind.

"Ma?" James asked suddenly, "would it be a'right for me to 'ave a rabbit? One to tame, I mean. I'd get its food and look after it. I didn't ask afore, 'cos we might 'ave 'ad t' eat it an' I wouldn't 'ave liked that. There's some little'ns down in bottom field—I could get one of them."

"Oh James, what are we goin' to do with yer. Give us time t' get used t' things first afore yer start thinkin' 'bout 'avin' animals." His mother sat down in the chair by the fire and shook her head slowly, not sure whether to laugh or cry.

The boy looked mortified. "Sorry ma. I'll ask pa later on, shall I?"

"Well, yer can, but just give 'im chance to get in the door first, will yer?" The woman chuckled.

There was laughter all round at this, from William included, although he did not really understand his brother's preoccupation with nature. As far as he was concerned James was welcome to go out in the cold morning air; he would rather have an extra hour's sleep in a warm bed—and to him, the best place for a rabbit was under a nice pastry crust.

The sound of laughter greeted their father as he came through the door, a widely smiling Arthur at his heels.

"What's all this then?" The sound of his voice brought a sudden hush to the room. But, to their astonishment, his face wore a smile too. It was like a dream, everyone smiling and all talking at once, where normally there was only the sound of logs crackling in the grate or the clatter of dishes to disturb the tiny room.

James wondered if being poor made people forget how to smile, but then he had a mental picture of Mr and Mrs Butler. They were poor but they smiled all the time.

As he roused himself from his thoughts, he saw his father looking at him.

"Anythin' wrong, lad?"

"No pa, I'm very pleased for yer and ... fer Arthur as well, but I'm..." He faltered not knowing how to finish the sentence. He was not even sure of what he wanted to say or how to put it into words.

"What is it?" His father frowned. He could not imagine what was troubling the boy.

"Nothin," the boy murmured lamely.

"Right, let's get some tea goin', shall we?" said Mrs Newland looking at Eliza, who to her amazement jumped up to help without having to be asked twice.

Tea over, James went outside to sit on the log-pile behind the cottage. He had found this a good quiet place to think, where he could look out across the fields to the wooded hillside, called the hanger. It was so peaceful, just a few cawing crows getting ready to roost for the night and the occasional 'cronk' from a pheasant up amongst the trees.

He tried to put his thoughts in order, but soon his mind wandered and he became immersed in his surroundings.

Approaching footsteps made him turn around. It was his father, probably come to get wood for the fire.

"I thought I'd find yer 'ere. One o' yer little spots ain't it?" James felt a shiver go through him; why was he nervous of his own father?

"James, I want to try and explain somethin' to yer. Yer may not understand; ye're still a mite young, but bright enough, so I'll try. Y' see, I know yer think yer ma an' me are 'ard on yer all. Per'aps we are a bit, but it's not easy with so many o' us an' so little money comin' into the 'ouse; we struggle on from one day to the next. It's got so's I've wondered 'ow t' go on sometimes.

"This new job's a godsend. We won't 'ave luxuries mind, but it'll make things easier, 'specially for yer ma. Y' see, our parents was much the same—it goes on from one generation to the next. Life don't really change out 'ere. But I'm 'opin' that per'aps yer can alter all that."

The boy looked at him warily. He had never heard his father make such a long speech, and what was more, something else seemed to be implied. He sat quietly, not knowing what to say.

Then his father chuckled, and James nearly fell off the logs. He hadn't heard his father laugh like that for a very long time.

"Ye're a popular lad yer know. Y've a way of understandin' things, knowing what's right some'ow, 'specially when it comes to

15

animals and plants and the like. Oh aye, folk 'oo knows yer says what a pleasant 'elpful lad yer are."

"William don't, 'e pinches me." James bit his lip; he hadn't meant to tell tales, it had just slipped out.

It didn't seem to worry his father. "Don't yer mind 'im, 'e's a mite jealous that's all. He's a nice enough boy but 'e's a bit clumsy and not so quick o' mind as y'self. It hasn't gone unnoticed 'round the village, as 'ow y' 'elp folk. Even Mr Turner 'as 'eard 'bout yer. 'Newland,' 'e says to me this mornin', 'I hear you have a youngster whose interested in animals and the countryside and is a hardworking kind of chap. I wonder if later on, when he's older, he would be interested in being apprenticed to my gamekeeper.'"

The boy's eyes grew wider as his father continued, "I think Mr Turner is pleased with the service our family 'as given 'is over the years, 'cos my pa worked for'n an' all, yer know." He paused. "Anyway the offer is there, although yer'll 'ave t' wait 'til ye're 'bout thirteen, but I'm sure time'll pass soon enough."

James looked at his father blankly for a moment as the news sunk in. A proper job when he left school and one which would keep him here in Selborne. He wondered if he was dreaming. Three years— quite a while to wait, but it would be worth it. He drew in a long breath. Just imagine going around all day with the gamekeeper, looking at the trees and flowers and birds. He was not sure what else a gamekeeper did, apart from walking around with his shotgun under his arm, so for now the dream stopped there.

"What do yer think lad? There'll be a lot to learn but I'm sure yer can do it—so does Mr Turner, otherwise 'e wouldn't 'ave offered yer the chance."

"Oh pa, I would like it more than anythin' else in the world."

His father smiled, "Right, I'll see Mr Turner as soon as I can. Meanwhiles, from what yer ma tells me, we'd better be gettin' yer some new boots. We'll go into Alton next Saturday. Yer'll 'ave t' promise me somethin' though, that yer won't go paddlin' in 'em."

James looked at his father, eyes big as saucers, and gulped. "She knew, didn't she. Ma knew what I'd done. I didn't paddle in 'em tho', only put me wet feet in 'em. Sorry pa."

His father chuckled again. "Oh she knew alright; we 'ad a good laugh 'bout it just now. Your face were a proper picture when yer came in this mornin', she told me."

James stared open mouthed. His parents. Having a laugh. Yesterday it would have seemed impossible, but now ... would there be no end to today's surprises. It must have shown on his face too.

Still smiling, his pa said, "Your ma an' me, we 'aven't always bin care-worn grown-ups yer know, we was young once an' all. My pa now, 'e would 'ave most likely given me a thrashin' if I'd done what yer did." He leant forward and ruffled his son's hair. "But enjoy bein' young while yer can lad. It won't be long afore yer grown into a man, an' then yer'll meet all of life's 'ardships soon enough."

James was having trouble coming to terms with the way his father seemed today. Was it just the thought of earning more money making a difference, or was it that he himself had never really known his parents, had only ever seen them as strict and abrupt, not realising that underneath they did care and that any discipline was only for their children's own good.

A sudden thought came to him. "Pa, I can't go into Alton next Saturday."

His father looked puzzled. "Why not, I thought yer'd 'ave jumped at the chance of new boots?"

"I'd like new boots, more 'an anythin', but yer see I've promised Mr Butler I'd 'elp 'im in 'is garden, an' I can't let 'im down."

"I see. Well, we can't 'ave yer lettin' anyone down can we; so we'll make it the followin' week, eh?" John Newland turned to go, then hesitated. "Just remember that me an' yer ma love yer, all on yer. In spite of all the 'ardship, we don't regret 'avin' any o' yer. When ye're older, there'll be things that we 'ave to tell yer, explain about. Things that 'appened a long time ago, but don't yer worry 'bout anythin' now, just stay as yer are. An' by the way, we'll talk 'bout a rabbit later." And with that his father left him.

James stayed sitting on the log-pile for quite a while in the gathering dusk, dreaming of the day when he could join the gamekeeper and spend his days strolling around the estate. It was something to look forward to, something to work and strive for. He thought about his new relationship with his parents and began to feel very grown-up.

As the light faded from the sky the boy still sat, knees hugged tightly to his chest.

It was a day he would remember for many years to come.

Chapter Two

James shivered and pulled the collar of his shabby jacket up around his neck. The early mist, instead of clearing, had become a light drizzle.

After waiting so impatiently for three years for this day to come, he wondered why he felt so nervous. It had all sounded so simple when his father had told him of Mr Turner's offer, but now that he was actually here...

He hoped Mr Harris would arrive soon. It had been the man's idea to meet here at daybreak, at the point where the fields gave way to a tree-covered hillside, but James had been waiting for what seemed like hours. It was quite chilly for late May too and as yet there were no birds on the wing nor tiny creatures about to entertain him. They were probably still tucked up snug and warm in nest or burrow.

He was feeling uncomfortably overdressed wearing Arthur's cast-offs, as they were still too big for him. The well-patched jacket covered his cotton shirt and the rough woollen material of his trousers chafed his skin, especially just below the knees where he had tied twine around his legs, to prevent anything small and furry going up any further. His boots were fine though; his father had insisted that he have a new pair and his feet were warm and dry.

At last he saw the gamekeeper coming along the lane towards him, a large man with a bristling black and grey streaked beard. He did not look over-pleased to see James, but the young man smiled, said, "Good morning, Mr Harris," and touched his forelock.

Mr Harris grunted. "Right Newland, all ready? let's get on then," and started off up the track leading into the trees. They passed through a gate which James closed carefully behind him. Better make a good impression, he thought. But the man strode on ahead without a word and his young apprentice could only follow in his wake, gazing at the big-framed figure with a leather-holstered shotgun slung across his back.

After a while they turned onto a narrow footpath heavily overhung with bushes and trees. The rain had become a downpour and soon James was soaked to the skin. He worried fleetingly about the bread and cheese for his lunch which was in his jacket pocket. His wet hair flopped over his face, causing rivulets of water to run down his face and off the end of his nose. With a cold hand he pushed the hair back. Where could they be going?

They came at last to a clearing, in the middle of which stood an enclosure of some kind. From inside this came the piping of young birds. James hurried forward and peered over the top of one of the hazel-wood hurdles. The sight which greeted him brought a wide smile to his face, all discomfort forgotten. Inside were about a hundred baby pheasants, falling over one another on still spindly legs—and the noise...

The boy was enchanted; guessing that they had come to feed them, he looked at Mr Harris, who had by now untied one of the hurdles and was stepping inside.

"Come on then, Newland. Don't just stand there, there's work to be done."

James sheepishly walked around to join him.

"Now," said the gamekeeper, "we've got to sort these birds out. Some of 'em is not up to scratch, see, like that one there." He pointed. "Now we can't 'ave them takin' space an' eatin' good food when it's obvious they ain't goin' to be no use. I'll do first one; it ain't very nice, but you'll soon get used to it."

To James' horror, the man grabbed the bird and swiftly wrung its neck, tossing the lifeless body over the hurdle. Then he turned towards his apprentice, who was by this time feeling sick, every nerve jangling with the certain knowledge of what was to come.

Mr Harris, seeing the boy's pallor, said, "It's got to be done. Do it quick, afore yer think too much 'bout it. That one there, 'e's pretty sickly."

Still the boy hesitated.

The man barked. "Go on, do it now."

And then James, who had never in his life, knowingly killed anything, gritted his teeth and made a grab for the tiny, feathered body. Shaking all over, he did what he had seen Mr Harris do, praying that he had done it right. It would be awful to cause the bird suffering.

He looked at the limp body in his hands.

Never. Never, would he get used to doing this sort of thing. Throwing the bird over the hurdle to join its sibling, James ran to the edge of the pen and retched.

Mr Harris did not seem in the least worried; perhaps he had seen it all before. He quickly sent two more of the hapless birds to their fate and then handed the boy an old sack saying, "'Ere, put 'em in that," and set about the business of feeding the lucky survivors. "You'll get used to it, lad. It's all in a day's work, this time of year anyway." Then he retied the hurdles. "Best get on."

They set off back along the pathway under the dripping trees, soon turning off again; this time there was no clear track, but the man seemed to know where he was heading.

In his mind James kept going over what had just happened. He hadn't dreamed that there would be such awful jobs to do. He realised that it must have been necessary otherwise Mr Harris would not have done it. Mr Turner was renowned for the shooting parties he gave every October, men coming from as far away as London to join in. Everyone said what a fine gamekeeper he had, what fine birds. To the youngster it was a bitter experience. To him it was a mystery why anyone would want to shoot the birds, or anything else for that matter, in the first place.

Mr Harris had stopped at a half-grown silver birch tree and was crouching over something on the ground. His assistant walked across to see what it was.

On the ground lay the body of a fox, a noose of thin wire pulled tightly around its neck. James caught his breath and swallowed hard.

"Poor thing."

The man swung around, "What do yer mean, poor thing. Bloody vermin, more like. This is one less to feed on me birds." So that was it, the poor animal had supposedly caught some of the young pheasants. To James' mind it was just as likely to be a magpie or a crow. It was the way of things.

"Put 'im in the bag an' all; we'll get rid of 'em when we get back to the office."

'Im? Didn't the man know anything. It was a female, not a male. James fumed. What if she had young? It was a little early in the year but you never knew; it had been a mild spring and sometimes the foxes mated early.

He gently placed the tawny body into the sack and then started peering and prodding under nearby bushes.

"What're yer doin'?" asked the man.

"Lookin' fer 'er lair. She might 'ave young'uns. They'll die if we leave 'em."

"Bloody good job too, bloody vermin," he said again, spitting on the ground as though to emphasise his words. "We've no time for that kind o' rubbish. Now, let's be gettin' on. I'm ready for me breakfast." So saying, Mr Harris stomped off the way they had come.

How could the man do that? just go off.

James was dumbfounded. Oh, what an awful morning; not a very good start to his working life that was sure. He knew everything had to die some time, it was all a part of life. Animals were killed for food every day. He had witnessed the slaughter of pigs and sheep at the farm and even enjoyed the end result. And Mr Turner's lovely hunting horse had been shot last year, watched tearfully by stable lads and grooms alike, but that had been different, the poor animal had broken his leg and was screaming in agony.

Today though, James thought the look on Mr Harris' face had been malicious. Was he perhaps not the kindhearted and friendly gamekeeper everyone thought so much of…?

Now he knew for sure that he would never like the man. He felt uncomfortable with him, a gut feeling. He was an odd person; apart from anything else he had hardly spoken a word, although to be fair he probably wasn't used to having anyone with him.

The years ahead did not look so rosy now.

Mr Harris had stopped again. They were just inside the copse, not far from the track along which they had first travelled. He picked up a stout stick and began prodding the earth around the base of a small fir tree. James watched, a frown creasing his brow. What was he looking for now?

Seemingly satisfied with whatever he had been checking, the gamekeeper straightened his back and set off again. Not one word passed his lips and the young would-be apprentice felt no desire to converse with so sullen a man, but hurried along behind him, his wet clothes chilling his body to the bone.

James suddenly realised what Mr Harris could have been looking for. A badger sett. There were several in the area. Surely the man would not harm them, there was no need. He decided that it might be an idea to keep an eye on that spot himself.

Now his immediate problem was what to tell his parents. They would be bound to ask how his day had gone. Should he lie and say all was well, or tell the truth? The situation would require a great deal of thought. And it wasn't even mid-morning yet. None too soon he saw the estate office ahead. Oh, for a hot drink and a little warmth!

Office was perhaps rather too grand a name for what was in reality a large wooden hut, but it was a welcome sight today.

After emptying his sack of dead creatures at the back where shown, James walked sadly around to the door, grateful to be getting in out of the rain. And for the first time that day he was not disappointed. It was warm and dry inside, with a large cast-iron stove puffing away in the corner and, standing in front of it, two old chairs with their stuffing hanging out. Somehow it managed to look almost cosy.

An enormous kettle bubbled away on top of the stove, its lid jumping up and down as though in some mad jig and, to the boy's surprise, Mr Harris quickly grabbed an old brown teapot, some tea from a caddy and had a brew made in minutes.

"Be your job usually, t' make tea, but I thought it'd be quicker t' do it meself today. What do yer think then—goin' t' like workin' with me?" The question caught James unawares.

"Uh, well ... I think so," he stammered. "We won't always 'ave t' kill things though, will we?"

The question hung in the air. Mr Harris shrugged. "We 'as to do what's necessary, it's estate management, that's what yer got t' learn. It don't 'appen every day o' course but this is the time o' year when there's a lot to sort out. Yer don't want t' worry so much 'bout animals, they don't 'ave feelin's same as us." James gritted his teeth and stayed silent. "Another day yer can get fed up t' back teeth o' mendin' fences." The shadow of a smile crossed the grizzled features, exposing blackened and broken teeth. "It takes many a long year t' learn it all, yeh, many a long year."

At that, he took a cloth-covered bundle from his pocket, unwrapped it and started eating with relish the bread and cheese it contained.

James pulled his own food from his sodden jacket. The clean cloth his mother had tied it up in was wet and stained with dye and he eyed it miserably. Inside, the bread was rather soggy but the cheese appeared to be edible. He realised sadly that there would not be enough food for two meals. So, should he eat it all now or try to save some for later? His rumbling stomach soon solved that little problem.

The hot, sweet tea was a real treat. James had to give the man his due there, he knew how to brew a good pot of tea. It washed the food down and left the boy feeling content, for a while.

Mr Harris did not talk much more, leaving his apprentice wondering what they were going to do next. Not more killing, he hoped.

Too soon it seemed, they were out in the damp air again. The cool breeze that blew along the hillside chilled their still-wet clothes; so much so, that James felt a longing to go straight home to his mother's cosy kitchen and a dish of her tasty broth.

They started checking the fencing which encircled the estate—to find any breaks which would allow hungry deer in, Mr Harris informed him. It seemed to run for miles and, fit though he was, James could feel his legs starting to ache. The only relief came when they stopped for lunch, which for him was just a mug of tea. Mr Harris seemed to have a never ending supply of food on him, but showed no inclination to share it although he must have realised that his companion had nothing left.

James longed for the day to be over, for more than one reason.

As the afternoon wore on the skies cleared, allowing fitful sunshine to brighten the day and spread enough warmth to stop him shivering, but when at last Mr Harris said, "Right, that'll do for t'day, we'll check rest o' fences tomorrer—see yer bright an' early at the office," the young man felt much relieved.

"Right. Bye, Mr Harris," was all he could manage.

Now, what should he do? Go home and get something to eat and change his clothes, or check on what had been worrying him all day?

His jacket and trousers were by this time almost completely dry. His decision made, he set off towards the copse where that morning they had found the body of the vixen. He had taken careful note of the surroundings and headed straight for the silver-birch.

Again and again he circled the area, crawling under bushes, scraping at leaf-mould—nothing. Then he widened his search, knowing that foxes cover quite a distance when looking for food. Further and further out amongst the trees he went, time forgotten, as was the gnawing in his gut. He felt compelled to carry on.

Suddenly he realised that the daylight was fading. He could not believe it, where had the time had gone? He had better get home—his parents would be worried. It was a shame though. He had felt certain that the vixen had cubs. Perhaps his instinct had been wrong.

James turned to make his way back to the track, but suddenly stopped. There it was again. A tiny sound, barely audible. He dropped to his knees and strained his ears, then, on all fours, crawled across to a nearby bush.

The weak, squealing call led him to a tiny hole hidden under protruding roots.

He had been right after all. Laying full stretch on his stomach he reached forward and by carefully parting grass and bramble shoots managed to lift out a mewling fox cub.

James guessed by its size, and the fact that its eyes weren't open, that it could not have been more than a week old. He placed the tiny animal inside his shirt to give it warmth and pushed his other hand down inside the hole to see if there were any more little bodies there, but could feel nothing.

He listened intently for a few more moments and then scrambled to his feet. Holding the precious bundle close, he set off in the gathering dusk towards his home.

Startled faces met him as he entered—his parents, brothers Arthur and William and two young sisters.

"Where on earth 'ave yer bin? an' look at the state o' yer," said his mother as she rose from her seat. "We've bin so worried—surely yer 'aven't bin workin' till this time?" She pulled her son to the chair that she had just vacated, "'Ere sit down, yer look all-in."

Her husband realised that his son held something inside his shirt, and reached out his hand. The other children sat silently at the table.

With stiff and trembling fingers, James gently lifted the tiny creature out onto the palm of his hand.

"Oh," cried Harriet, "look Lizzie, isn't 'e sweet?" The girls crowded round as their father took the animal from his son. "Is it still alive?" asked Eliza, reaching forward to stroke it with one finger.

"Let me get to the light." Mr Newland crossed the tiny room in one stride and peered at the cub by the glow from the candle. He turned to his youngest son. "I'm sorry lad, 'e's dead. Too young to leave its ma, I s'pose. Tell us what 'appened; 'ow did yer come t' find 'im?"

"I think as 'ow we'd better get the boy out o' them damp clothes an' somethin' warm inside 'im afore we start askin' questions, don't you?" Ann Newland cut in, her concern for her son being uppermost in her mind, "an' you girls 'ad better be gettin' off t' bed an' all. Go on, up yer go."

James' sisters turned reluctantly towards the staircase. "Eliza, drop one o' the blankets down, will yer, please." Their mother brooked no argument.

William sat grinning and nudging Arthur, who in turn frowned back at him, but one look from their father put a stop to any trouble.

"Now, son, tell us." John Newland sat down opposite his son, while his wife busied herself ladling hot broth into a bowl.

"'Ere, get them clothes off yer, an' wrap the blanket 'round yerself," she said, "before yer 'ave this."

James undressed, embarrassed by the close proximity of his two brothers, and pulled the rough woollen cover tightly around his shoulders. It felt good to be out of his clothes, and soon the soothing warmth of the broth seeped through him.

He was glad when, at last, his father sent the older boys off to their beds. They were clearly disappointed at having to miss his story, but would not dare defy their parents. William threw James a look of disdain which let the boy know that he would be ribbed mercilessly as soon as it was possible.

Once they had gone, the would-be apprentice gamekeeper, told his parents about his first day at work. It was not a very detailed account, the warm fire and the broth doing nothing to help him fight off his exhaustion, but his father and mother knew their son well enough to fill in any blanks.

They looked at one another, perplexed.

James saw this and tried to reassure them, "I'll be alright. It just takes a bit o' gettin' used to, that's all. I won't let yer down, I promise."

His mother smiled, "We know yer won't, son. Come on, off to yer bed. Y' need yer sleep. Meanwhile, I've got to find yer somethin' to wear for tomorrer."

"Could I have a little more broth first, please ma?"

"Course yer can, son. 'Ere, I'll get it." His mother filled the bowl once more, then glanced towards her husband, "Are yer goin' t' put that outside?" she pointed to the dead cub.

"Yeh, I'll see to 'im." He turned. "Now don't yer worry son, I'm sure everything'll be alright."

"Thanks, pa." The boys eyes were drooping with tiredness and once the last drop of broth had been cleaned from his bowl, he hauled himself up the stairs to the room overhead which he had to share with the other children.

He prayed that William would be asleep; he could not take any of his brothers mockery tonight. But James never knew—the only sound he heard before sleep swept over him, was the quiet breathing of his siblings. His slumbers brought about a strange mixture of dreams; fox cubs, pheasant chicks and ... soggy bread.

Chapter Three

The following day was considerably more undemanding for James. The sun shone, he had plenty of food and Mr Harris seemed to be in a more amenable mood. They spent the morning checking the rest of the fences and looking in on the pheasant chicks, none of whom—to James' relief—had to be disposed of. He wondered if perhaps it was the better weather that had caused the improvement in the game-keeper's temper. Today, the man had been almost chatty and interested in what the boy thought about the countryside, even helping him with the names of some of the more obscure plants.

His heart lifted. This was more how he had expected things to be. Mending a fence here, cutting back the encroaching ferns there and all the while birds soared overhead, filling the countryside with song. Even finding a dead pigeon, its crop torn apart, could not dampen his spirits. The woodland brought its own pungent smells. New, green bracken shoots springing up through rotting branches and thick layers of last year's leaf mould all wove their magic. A few pale primroses peeked out into the dappled light, and when they came upon a carpet of bluebells cutting a swathe through the trees the heady perfume overpowered everything else. To his eyes nothing could ever better the sight of trees in spring, dressed veil-like in fresh green foliage, and the hedgerows coming to life with a myriad of bright flowers.

The afternoon spent in the office was not so much to James' liking, but, as Mr Harris pointed out, the paperwork was important as well. This was not good news for the youngster, books and the like not being his strong point. In fact, even writing his name caused him problems. Perhaps he could learn, but the prospect was daunting. In the meantime he took out one of Mr Turner's labrador dogs, which had been left in their care—a rare and enjoyable treat for the boy; and he wondered if ma and pa would consider having a dog….

Soon it was time to go home, and today it was a much happier young man who set off in the warm sunshine.

Jacket swinging jauntily from one finger, he strode along the lane, and when after a while he saw his brother ahead of him with two friends, he hurried forward to tell them of his day at work.

But the moment he saw William's face, James knew that he was in for a rough time. The older boy and his cronies started whispering earnestly and laughing loudly as he drew nearer, then they set about teasing and taunting him.

"'Ere 'e is, the soppy sod. Not found any babbies t'day then?" This from William. The other boys laughed even louder at that, then joined in a jeering chant.

"Dopey, dopey, dopey Newland." They called. Then one sneered. "Nursin' babbies is fer girls. Yer soppy, yer are."

They made a ring around him and carried on with the jibes.

James tried to make them understand, "It were only a cub, 'is ma was dead. 'E 'ad to 'ave 'is chance."

But it was no good—if anything it made them worse—and when at last he decided that flight would a better alternative, they started pushing him from one to another, getting rougher and rougher with every shove.

All the while William taunted, "Bet yer cried, didn't yer. Proper cry-baby yer are. Cry-baby, cry-baby."

Pushed to the limit, James shouted at William, "Yer only jealous, 'cause you 'aven't got a proper job. Yer too thick an' no one likes yer."

Silence hung on the still air. The village boys flicked their eyes nervously from one brother to the other and waited, with bated breath, for what was no more than a few seconds.

With a roar of rage, William lashed out, knocking his slighter-built brother to the ground with a single punch. The other boys quickly joined in, kicking the figure on the ground. Blow after blow rained down, knocking the breath out of him, and dust flew into his eyes and mouth making him choke—then just when he thought he could bear no more, they stopped.

The sound of pounding feet filled his ears, merging with the sound of his thudding heart as he painfully opened one eye. His three attackers were running off towards the village as though the devil himself were after them, and painfully turning his head to look in the opposite direction he saw why. Two women were approaching. One he vaguely recognised from the village, although he could not think of her name. They were deep in conversation, but at the sight of the boy in front of them, stopped aghast.

"Good 'eavens, what's 'appened to you? Are you alright?" one of them asked.

Her companion tut-tutted. "Someone's set on 'im, poor little chap. Shall we see you 'ome, son?"

27

James dragged himself to his feet. "N-no, I-I'm alright, thanks. It isn't far. Th-thanks anyway." And he stumbled off along the lane without a backward glance.

Reaching the cottage, he peered cautiously around the doorway. To his relief the kitchen was empty. Pain seared through his body as he made for the stairs and climbed them with difficulty. Once in the upper room he sat down heavily on the nearest bed to wait for his head to stop spinning. He looked in despair at his clothes. Apart from his jacket, which had not been torn but was extremely dusty, they were a mess. His shirt and breeches were in tatters and he wailed inwardly. What was his mother going to say?

He looked around the cramped room for something to wear. There was an old shirt hanging behind the door, that would have to do for now. He removed the remnants of the shirt that he had been wearing, every movement making him wince. The clean garment felt cool against his burning skin, but now he did not know what to do with his trousers. He pulled ineffectually at the torn material; perhaps he could say it had happened at work.

Suddenly he was aware of movement downstairs and hauled himself to his feet to see who it was. He crept slowly a little way down the wooden stairway, then let out a sigh of relief. It was his mother, but she was busy at the sink washing vegetables and without looking around, said, "Is that you, James? Mr Butler would like some firewood chopped, if yer don't mind, son. Everythin' alright t'day, eh?"

"Yeh, alright thanks ma. I won't be long, then." James managed to speak from between rapidly-swelling lips.

"Good boy. I'll be gettin' yer dinner on," Mrs Newland said, scrubbing earth from the fresh-dug carrots and not noticing her son cross painfully to the door.

Once out in the fresh air James felt a little better and made his way the short distance down the lane to Honeysuckle Cottage. He liked helping the Butlers, they had always been kind to him, and over the years he had come more and more often to their cottage to do odd jobs for them.

He trudged up their pathway and prepared to make his way around to the back, but as he passed the open front door Mrs Butler called out to him.

"Ah, here's our James, come in lad, come in."

"I'd better not Mrs Butler," he said, peering into the dim interior, "I'm pretty dusty."

As his eyes adjusted to the gloom, he saw a young girl and touched his forelock politely.

"This is our granddaughter, Mary Ann. She's over on a visit from Froyle." Mr Butler said proudly. "I don't think you've met afore."

James was not really interested in girls, his giggling sisters being enough to put anyone off. But he had to admit, even in his weakened state, Mr Butler did indeed have something to be proud of. She had glossy, dark-brown hair which curled around her pale face, and clear blue eyes, rather like those of her grandmother.

He gripped the doorframe and tried not to stare. "Afternoon Miss. I-I'll get round the back now." He managed to utter this as giddiness threatened to overcome him again, and then left as fast as his feeble state would allow. It would be too embarrassing to pass out in front of a girl.

Mr Butler had left out some logs which James guessed were to be chopped into kindling, and picking up the axe he set about his task, but before long he had to stop and sit down on the chopping block, head in hands, waiting for the dizziness to pass.

How long he sat there he was never sure, but suddenly arms were around his shoulders and he was being helped into the kitchen. From what sounded like a long way off, Mrs Butler's voice reached him, insisting that he tell them who had done this dreadful thing. She brushed her hand gently across his forehead and pushed damp hair out of his eyes, all the while making soothing noises.

James was at first aware of Mr Butler's presence, but then he seemed to go.

"I've sent 'im off to get your ma an' pa," said Mrs Butler, as though sensing his thoughts. "Don't you fret, we'll look after you. My, my just look at these bruises. Oh, you poor boy, someone 'as got to be wicked to do this."

He tried to protest. They mustn't find out who did it—William would only bully him all the more if he thought that he'd split on him. But words would not come, his swollen mouth and bruised jaw prevented any movement, and his vision was blurred with the flesh puffed up around his eyes.

Suddenly he felt sick. Luckily Mrs Butler had been prepared for this and pushed a white enamel bowl in front of him, and once the worst was over she gently placed cooling, damp clothes around his searing head.

Vaguely, he heard his mother come in through the door. Her loud gasp was the last thing he remembered before a thick, grey mist swirled in and overtook him.

"Ah, decided to join us again 'ave yer?" His mother's face smiled down at him.

Where was he? James tried to lift his head from the pillow, but the pain was excruciating.

"Ma, 'ow long 'ave I bin 'ere?" He was in his own bed and bright sunlight shone through the tiny window.

"Nearly two days," she said, stroking his head, much as he remembered Mrs Butler doing. It was very soothing. Slowly, everything started coming back to him. He looked at his mother determined to explain to her what had happened, but she shook her head.

"Don't try to speak yet, yer still too poorly. I'll go an' get yer some broth, see if yer can manage a drop." Then, standing up, she gently patted his shoulder and went quietly downstairs.

He must have dozed, because almost immediately his mother reappeared holding a small bowl. "'Ere we are son, try some o' this." She lifted his head a little and placed another pillow underneath. "There, that should make it easier. Are yer comfy?"

Stiffness prevented James from nodding, so he murmured that he was, and his mother placed a spoonful of the liquid to his lips. The broth trickled down his throat, tasty and warming. He indicated that he would like some more, but after that, his strength failed him.

"Never mind, son. Yer've done well considerin'. Now, get some rest, yer'll feel better as time goes on." She pulled the sheet up under his chin and brushed his cheek with her finger tips. "Sleep is what yer need more than anythin'. I'll be up later with a mug o' tea, alright?" She smiled and left him.

James fretted. He must try to explain. Why wasn't ma cross about his clothes? His head hurt from thinking, so he closed his eyes. The picture of a girl swam into focus, a girl with blue eyes. She was lovely… He dozed again.

It was dark when he next awoke, but the murmur of voices rising from the kitchen below told him that his parents were still up, so it could not be too late in the evening. A few moments later candlelight lit up the room as his mother reached the top of the stairs.

"Are you awake?" she whispered.

"Yes ma, I am." He took the mug of tea which she offered and managed to sip it through his still-swollen lips. "I feel a bit better, can I get up?"

"Oh, James, you're nowhere near well enough to get up. Yer covered in bruises an' the doctor said yer was to rest yer 'ead for several more days yet. It were a very bad beatin', yer know." She sat down on the bed and took one of his hands in hers. "Yer lucky not to 'ave any permanent damage, doctor says." She smiled tenderly at her son, "My poor boy, all that just for rescuin' a fox cub."

James was astonished. How did she know that?

His mother took a deep breath. "We know what 'appened, son. Just after yer'd left to go to the Butlers, Miss Jessop from the village called in to see 'ow yer were. She and 'er friend was surprised yer weren't 'ere after the state they'd seen yer in. Just then Mr Butler arrived to say yer was poorly, so we all 'urried down to Honeysuckle Cottage t' fetch yer back 'ere." She paused, "I 'ad the shock of me life when I saw yer. Thought yer was dead. So did our Will. When 'e came in an' saw yer, 'e were so frightened, thinkin' 'e killed yer, 'e told us everythin'. That young man won't be sittin' down fer a while—yer father gave 'im a right leatherin' I can tell yer." She looked at her son thoughtfully, 'E's gone to stay with yer brother Fred an' 'is wife, 'til we think e's ready to come 'ome."

And then, to reassure him, "By the way, yer pa went to see Mr Harris an' explained what 'appened, so don't worry 'bout yer job, everything's alright." She smiled fondly. "Now, do yer want anythin' else?"

His head reeled, from shock as well as from injury. Fancy William owning up. "I think I'll be alright, ma, thanks. Is pa cross with me?"

"Why would yer pa be cross with you?" She asked. "Nobody's cross. We're all upset that it 'appened. Pa'll be up in a few minutes, so 'e can see for 'imself 'ow yer doin'. G'night son—see yer in the mornin'."

A little later his father came upstairs and seated himself on the bed. "'Ow are yer now?" he asked kindly. "Yer face is a pretty sight, I can tell yer. Good job we ain't got any mirrors, yer'd frighten yer-self." He laughed at the unaccustomed joke, but James felt that the merriment was hiding a worry. "I didn't realise 'ow bad things were between you and yer brother. 'As 'e always picked on yer so bad?"

James decided to be honest with his father. "Well, 'e didn't used to be as bad as 'e is now, but since 'e started labourin' fer that chap at

Empshott 'e's got worse. I 'eard 'im tellin' Arthur that the other men workin' there make fun of 'im 'cos of 'is nose, an' 'im bein' a bit slow. Do yer think that's why 'e picks on me?"

William had a nose which tended to be a little over-large and sometimes had a bluey tinge, especially in winter.

John Newland stroked his chin and murmured, "I see. Yer could be right, son. I'll 'ave a word with 'im afore 'e comes 'ome. 'Cos we're so used to it, we don't notice 'is nose, but I 'spose others do. Not fair if they rib 'im though—weren't 'is fault it 'appened."

James was about to ask how it had happened, but his father rose to go. "See yer in the mornin'—'ope yer can get a bit o' sleep. Night."

"Night, pa." He eased himself into a more comfortable position, feeling sure that he would be unable to sleep after dozing all day, and thought about the happenings of the past few days. There had certainly been a few surprises, but something worried him more than anything else and kept nagging at the back of his mind. And just as he slid into a fitful sleep he realised what it was—had Mary Ann seen him when he was sick and unconscious? He did hope not.

Chapter Four

James felt strong enough to return to work. His parents were still worried about him, but, knowing that he had never been one to stay idle indoors for long, gave in to his request to do so.

Although the bruises on his face and neck had faded considerably, his ribs were still a patchwork of ugly red weals. He knew that his looks would never win him any prizes, and had worried in case Mary Ann was still staying with her grandparents. But then, he told himself, she would never glance at him twice anyway, and he was cross at his own thoughts. What did he want with the attentions of girls?

It was good to get back out into the fresh air, and as he filled his lungs, James knew that this was the best way to spend his time, tramping the woods and fields with Mr Harris. To his surprise, the man had shown great concern over his beating, and this brought the two closer together. It also altered some of his earlier views about him and his methods.

A few weeks later, however, a gradual change in the gamekeeper's manner became apparent, and he reverted to his sarcastic and taciturn self which had been so evident on that first day. For a while James tried hard to ignore the caustic remarks, but after an exceptionally trying day when Mr Harris had spent every working hour in the office staring morosely at the stove, James patience finally ran out. He knew that there were urgent things to be done out on the estate—one fence in particular needed mending—and so he went off to see to it himself, and prayed that he had done the job properly. It would be disastrous if the deer wandered in and ate their fill of the fresh green shoots. And what was worse he, James, would most likely get the blame.

On his way home later, he met one of the lads from the stables with whom he had become friendly and vented his frustration.

"Oh, back on the juice, is 'e," said the lad, whose name was Tom. He was two years older than James and seemed very grown-up and knowledgeable to the younger boy.

"The what?" James looked puzzled.

"The juice, the beer, the drink—you know…" Tom shrugged. "'E used to be in trouble a while ago due to 'is drinkin'. Mr Turner

33

warned 'im 'e'd get the push if it 'appened again. Stupid if yer ask me, wastin' yer 'ard earned cash in the pub."

James agreed. "I've never bin in one, don't think me pa 'as either. What do yer think I should do 'bout Mr Harris, then?"

Tom scratched his head with a callused finger, his brown eyes thoughtful. "Well ... don't rightly know. Yer can't really go runnin' to Mr Turner, can yer? Perhaps yer pa'd know, 'e's worked for the boss a long time." He pulled his cap back on at a rakish angle and said, "Ah well, I must be gettin' 'ome to me tea—see yer soon." Then he strode off along the lane, whistling as he went.

James thought hard as he walked on. Tom was right—telling his father seemed like the only thing to do. It did seem so disloyal though, and on reflection he decided not to say anything just yet. He would see how Mr Harris was for a few more days. The man could not drink every night surely—his wage would not be large enough for that, even though he lived in a tied cottage and had no family to support.

But the situation did not improve; in fact it got worse.

James became more and more worried about work being left undone. He did what he could, but was severely limited through lack of experience. Fences were not too much of a problem—he was getting quite good at them—but he knew that there must be other things which needed doing.

"Yer lookin' a bit fed-up t'night, son," his father remarked one evening as they worked together in the garden.

James stopped weeding and leaned on his hoe. "To tell the truth, pa, I've got somthin' of a problem."

"Oh, ar, what's that then?" His father wiped the sweat from his brow with a dusty forearm and sat himself on the saw-horse to listen.

"It's Mr 'Arris—'e's not doin' much work, an' 'e's in a terrible temper most of the time. Any idea's on what I can do pa?"

John Newland let out a low whistle. "'E's a stupid man. 'E were told a year ago it were 'is last warnin'." He stared thoughtfully at the cabbages as though they might give him inspiration. "I'm not sure what we should do son, but leave it with me an' I'll think 'bout it." Then he looked at his son through narrowed eyes. "'Ow long 'as this bin goin' on?"

"Couple o' weeks now. I'm doin' what I can, but it ain't much." The boy looked downcast. "Tom told me the problem, pa. Drink ain't no good is it?"

"No son, it ain't. I'm glad none o' me sons seems to 'ave taken to it—brings nothin' but trouble." Something in his voice caused James to glance up sharply.

"Yer don't drink, do yer pa?"

"No, not now." He rose from his seat, "Right, we'd better get on with this—light's failin'. Yer leave worryin' 'bout Mr 'Arris to me."

His reply left the boy with some unanswered questions, but now was obviously not the time to ask, and so with a deep sigh James carried on with his battle against the weeds.

The following evening, while sawing logs for Mr Butler, James looked up to see Mary Ann standing at the open doorway watching him. He had been unaware that she was visiting, and seeing her there so suddenly sent a shock-wave through him. This was the first time that he had seen her since the day of his beating. He'd been glad to know that she'd not seen him in that battered state—Mrs Butler had chuckled merrily and reassured him when he had asked her about it.

Now, he could feel a flush slowly creeping across his face. How long had she been standing there? He nodded to her and stammered, "E-evenin' miss."

She smiled, but it was rather with her eyes than her mouth. James thought that she seemed rather distant—perhaps she enjoyed watching common labourers work up a sweat. Then, before he could think of anything else to say, she turned and disappeared into the cottage.

He felt disappointment wash over him, and started sawing again with renewed vigour. Why should he worry about her, she was only a child anyway. Couldn't be more than nine or ten years old. What was the matter with him?

He finished his chores, then called out his goodbyes to the elderly couple and set off for a walk. It was a lovely evening, warm and tranquil. Here and there a few small white butterflies danced around the flowering vetch by the hawthorn hedge, and a blackbird trilled out its song to a mate in the old apple tree at the rear of his parents cottage. He felt light-hearted and let his feet find their own direction. It didn't matter which way he went. The village was as familiar to him as his own hand and the desire to spend the whole of his life here had never diminished—Selborne was home.

He found himself taking the pathway along the edge of the copse near to where he had spent that first awful day at work, and on an impulse decided to check the area for signs of badgers or foxes. More of them would have had young by now and, although still not grown enough to leave the safety of their home, he might be lucky and see some today. He thought longingly of his little foundling and the trouble it had caused him. He smiled—it would not stop him from doing the same again.

Then the smile froze on his face.

There, in the spot where he had seen Mr Harris prodding the ground all those weeks ago, was a large hole. He ran across to it, dropped to his knees and peered in. It was obvious that it had been dug out by men with shovels, not by animals. It was far too big for one thing, and the excavated soil was heaped mostly to one side.

Rage replaced his feelings of pleasure. He knew what had happened here and he did not like it. Badger baiting was illegal, but still went on from time to time. To James, it was both cruel and barbaric.

He jumped to his feet and raced homeward. Many thoughts rushed through his mind, jostling for space. The one awful thing which kept pushing to the fore was—Mr Harris. Did he know about it? Had he something to do with it?

James tried to keep an awful premonition at bay. His relief when he saw his father working in the garden was enormous. "Pa," he panted. "Pa," and tears welled up.

John Newland looked up in alarm, and almost ran to meet the boy. "What is it, son?"

In between gasps for breath, James told his father of his find up in the copse.

"Oh, no, not another one. There's bin several setts found dug up 'round 'ere in the past few weeks. 'Course, if Mr 'Arris 'ad bin doin' 'is job proper, yer'd 'ave known." John Newland rubbed a grimy hand over his stubbly chin. "I'd best go an' see Mr Turner first thing tomorrer. Yer'd better show me where 'tis."

"Why do they do it pa?" asked James as they walked back along the track, "I can't understand it. Killin' fer killin's sake, 'tis awful."

"Money, that's what they do it for. No, yer'd never understand son, but there are folk as 'ud pay for the sport of watchin' them poor animals pulled apart. Sport?" he spat the word out. "There're some strange people in this world son, people I 'ope yer never 'as to meet nor deal with."

As James and his parents sat quietly in the kitchen later on that evening and Mrs Newland was told about the find, the boy blurted out his misgivings about the possible involvement of Mr Harris. He had not been sure whether to voice his worry or not, but now it seemed the right thing to do.

To his surprise his father did not argue with his thinking. "Could be the reason for 'is bad temper. If 'e's 'ad extra money fer drink, it'd be showin' itself that way. It's a bad business, anyways."

The following morning James arrived at work to find that Mr Harris was not anywhere to be seen, and a little later Mr Turner arrived at the estate office.

"Morning Newland. I thought it best to tell you myself that Mr Harris is no longer in my employ. Now, until I get a new gamekeeper I am getting someone over from Lord Percival's estate to look after things. He will arrive later today, so if you would like to wait here for him..." Mr Turner laughed, "Even show him a thing or two I shouldn't wonder. You are doing well, young man, very pleased with you and the way you tried to carry on, most commendable." He doffed his cap and strode off towards his waiting horse.

James stood rooted to the spot. How had anyone known about that? He wondered disconsolately where Mr Harris had gone, because although he had not liked the man too much, they had been getting along so much better recently.

Later, his father filled him in on all the details. It had been two things happening at once that had brought about the gamekeepers downfall.

"As I was waitin' to see Mr Turner this mornin', one of the groom's was tellin' me that 'e'd seen Mr 'Arris in a pub over at Empshott last evenin' an' 'e was throwin' money around 'an treatin' everyone to drinks. 'E 'ad a few shifty lookin' fellers with 'im an' when they left the pub, Sid the groom, an' 'is mate followed 'em outside." He paused to get his breath, "When they saw 'em settin' off towards the woods, with five dogs as 'ad bin outside, they were even more suspicious, an' trailed 'em to see what they was up to. Sure enough, they went straight to woodland over towards Newton way where 'e knew there was several setts." John Newland shook his head, "Well, Sid didn't 'ang around. 'As 'e said, 'e didn't want to see nothin' like that. Anyway, we decided to go in an' see Mr Turner together." He let out a low whistle, "Cor, 'oppin' mad 'e were—went straight round to 'Arris's 'ouse an confronted 'im. I 'eard as 'ow 'e 'ad to shake the man awake—still in a stupor apparently. But 'e confessed, came straight out with it, an' got thrown out on 'is ear.

Serves the blighter right." He sat back and drew on his clay pipe with satisfaction. "Good riddance, I say."

James looked at his parents in dismay, "I'll 'ave to get used to a new bloke now. 'Ope 'e's alright." Then to his father he said, "Mr Turner's nice ain't 'e? I 'adn't met 'im afore. Seemed to know a lot about me though." He paused. "Does 'e ask 'bout me, pa?"

"Oh, we chat sometimes, son," his father smiled. "We 'ave known each other fer a good few years yer know. 'E was good to me when I needed 'elp."

The boy was curious, but his father would say no more, pointing out that it was time for bed and anyway he was too young to know of such things.

As he climbed the stairs, James said very seriously, "I shan't ever drink ale pa, not if it makes yer do 'orrible things." He reached the top and turned to look down at his parents, just in time to see a look of intense understanding pass between them.

His father smiled again. "That's nice to know son. We're pleased about that aren't we mother?"

Ann Newland replied softly, "Very pleased," and she was looking at her husband with a smile which brightened the room.

James lay in his bed and thought how nice it must be to have someone smile at you like that. Will it ever happen to me he wondered?

A few weeks later his world changed dramatically. The new game-keeper employed by Mr Turner had stated firmly that he did not want —in his own words—a snotty-nosed kid following him around all day. Mr Turner was very sorry, but the man had come with excellent references and good gamekeepers were hard to come by. Would young master Newland like to work in the stables instead?

Young master Newland did not need asking twice.

Chapter Five

The stallion's coat gleamed like molten-gold in the April sunshine and James stepped back to admire his handiwork. Sorrento was the most magnificent horse in the stables and as today was the annual Greatham Stag Hunt, Mr Turner would expect his mount to be immaculate.

He strode into the stable-yard and came to stand beside stableboy and horse. "Morning Newland."

"Mornin' sir." James touched his forelock. But his employer only had eyes for Sorrento.

"Ah, you look marvellous old boy, absolutely top class." He rubbed the velvet nose and as usual his trusty friend snorted and pricked his ears in answer. "I must say you've done a good job on him, Newland."

"Thank you, sir." Pride swelled the young man's chest as he handed Mr Turner the reins and cupped hands for him to mount. Sitting tall in the saddle and looking resplendent in his hunting pink, Mr Turner gave a brief salute before easing the powerful beast into a canter as they swung into the lane.

James watched them go, wistfully praying that one day he would get the chance to ride the horse, and hurried across to the tack room, where his friend Tom was working,

"Get away alright?" Tom asked, as he buffed up a brass snaffle.

"Yeh, 'e were real pleased with 'is turn-out—said so," the younger man boasted. "'Ere, what yer tryin' to do, see yer ugly mug in that?"

"Better'n your'n. An' show a bit more respect fer yer elders, will yer?" Tom threw a cloth at his friend. The difference in their ages was a running joke between them. It helped to relieve the long working hours as they carried out the never-ending tasks of cleaning tack, mucking-out and exercising horses.

James had never for one moment regretted coming to work at the stables. He had been here nearly four years now and had fitted in from the start, enjoying the work and quickly learning to ride. He could not imagine ever doing anything else. His only disappointment was that he could not ride Sorrento, but no one was allowed on his back except Mr Turner.

It was not a large stable—only a dozen horses—and apart from himself and Tom there were two other stable-lads, Fred and Joe, and they all got along fine. There was also a taciturn man called Sam who drove Mrs Turner's carriage. He was arrogant, aloof and lazy, and no one really liked him.

The stable manager was Mr Bates who was a hard taskmaster with a sharp tongue. Although no one could fault his work—Mr Turner was known to have the best run stables in the area—the staff were put through difficult times to achieve it. Often they worked late into the evening as punishment because one of them had supposedly been slacking during the day, but on the whole it was a happy workplace; not least because Mr Turner himself was a good and respected employer.

From the very first day James had been shown the ropes by Tom, the two had formed a strong bond and become firm friends. There had been plenty to learn; not just about the tack, but the feed and mucking-out and, one of his favourite jobs, grooming the horses. He had been an able and willing pupil, quickly learning everything from his friend's expert tuition.

The new gamekeeper, who had put a stop to James' previous ambition, still worked on the estate and did the job far more efficiently than Mr Harris ever had. There was no animosity between them though, because the boy had made it quite clear that he was much happier in the stables anyway.

Life at home was easier too. Apart from himself, there were only his two younger sisters living in the cottage with their parents. William had settled well to life on a farm at nearby Blackmoor and lived in with a family there, and Arthur was happily doing the same thing at Newton. William and James had become more friendly as the years went by, even going off to a local pub for an ale or two— unbeknown to their parents.

Tom put down the brush he had been using and stretched his sturdy body. "I've seen enough o' them things for t'day, don't know 'bout you." He yawned loudly.

"Late night?" James enquired.

"Nah, not really. I went to see Laura's pa."

"Oh yeh, 'ow did yer get on?" He had forgotten that his friend was going to ask for the girl's hand. "So, when's the 'appy day?"

"Not yet awhiles, 'er pa says we've to wait two years. I ask yer, two bloody years. I'll be in me dotage by then."

James laughed at his friend's expression. "It'll soon pass, yer'll see. Laura's young yet, ain't she?"

"Yeh, only sixteen. I can see 'er pa's point." He sighed, "'E told me as 'ow 'e'd kill me if I touched 'er afore then. Huh, as if I would." He sounded so indignant that James cast him a sharp glance, but Tom's face told a different story, his brown eyes were alight with merriment and a saucy grin spread from ear to ear.

James said nothing, but couldn't help wondering—just what had the young couple been up to.

"You still not courtin'?" Tom asked.

"Nah, can't be bothered."

"What sort of excuse is that? Yer don't know what yer missin' man." Tom tutted to himself and, picking up his cloth and brush, set to work once more. But the grin never left his face.

The two young men worked on in companionable silence, while James thought over what his friend had said. He knew it was true. He was missing out, but try as he might he could not get Mary Ann out of his thoughts. If he could not have her, then he would go without.

He had seen her many times over the years and each occasion had confirmed his feelings for her. Although she now smiled warmly at him, there was never a hint of anything more. She was still young, and probably not even interested in boys yet.

He had found out a lot about her from Mrs Butler, who loved to talk about the girl. She was the daughter of Mr and Mrs Butler's only child, Charlotte Knight, who appeared to be a widow. Mother and daughter lived in a cottage in the village of Froyle, which was about nine miles away. Even though there was no Mr Knight, mother and daughter were always well dressed; which led James to assume that they had been left amply provided for. He knew that he must look like a tramp in their eyes, and this caused him considerable discomfort.

He had last seen Mary Ann about three weeks ago at Honeysuckle Cottage. He had been doing some work for Mr Butler, sitting astride the roof making good some brickwork on the chimney-stack, when she emerged from the cottage door below. Her dark brown, curly hair shone in the sunlight and her dress of white muslin gave her, in his eyes, the look of an angel. She had been followed by an older woman and James remembered hoping fervently that this sour-faced person was not her mother. He had dismissed the idea on the premise that Mr and Mrs Butler would never have produced such a miserable offspring.

"Mornin' Mary Ann. Mornin' ma'm." He called down to them.

The girl gave him a smile that gladdened his heart, but the woman just glared and hurried off down the lane, calling to the girl to hurry up.

Later on, as he had returned the ladder to the back of the cottage, he had seen Mrs Butler at her scullery window.

"'Ello lad, all finished. Do us a few years yet, will it?" she asked. "I'm right grateful to yer, that I am. I don't know what we'd 'ave done without yer over the past few months. Mr Butler's not able to do these things 'isself now. Yer a grand lad, yer are—always 'ave bin."

James had squirmed in embarrassment at the profuse praise, but there had been only one thing he wanted to know.

"Er ... I saw Mary Ann leavin' just now. Friend of 'er's with 'er, were it?" He had hardly dared to ask.

"Oh, bless yer lad, that were 'er ma, our Charlotte." She had chuckled, "I forgot yer'd not met 'er afore. Just off 'ome they were."

James remembered how his heart had sunk into the very soles of his boots. Now he was abruptly hauled back to the present by the sound of Tom's voice.

"'Ere yer'll wear that bridle out if yer rub it any 'arder. I 'ope she's worth it." The man was eyeing him with curiosity. Tom didn't know James' secret—no one did—but it didn't stop him guessing.

James laughed, "What do yer mean?"

"Oh, come on, I know that look. Yer can't fool me." His friend's face creased in the familiar smile. "Are yer affections returned?"

"I very much doubt it," James said sadly. He felt that Tom wouldn't understand even if he explained the situation to him. He was so much more confident and had an easy way with girls. His sturdy build, cheerful nature and laughing eyes were enough to set many a female heart fluttering. "Anyway, she don't know I exist." He managed a lop-sided grin, "And no, I'm not tellin' yer 'oo she is."

"Up to you, but I bet yer tell me afore long." Tom always had to have the last word.

They trudged across the yard to the little room at the end of the block where a wood-burning stove was used to boil the kettle and where they could sit and eat their food.

Mr Bates had his in his office—usually accompanied by the churlish Sam, unless he was out driving Mrs Turner.

The men had only a short break—just time to drink a mug of scalding tea and shove a hunk of bread down—before they were hard at work again. James' next task was to muck out Sorrento's loose-box, while Tom went into the next to see to Solomon, a bay gelding who had once held the exalted position now enjoyed by the younger hunter.

He was a very gentle animal and now, in his later years, was used mainly by Mr Turner's sons for hacking or to run errands. Solomon and Tom had a special affinity, and James could hear the man now talking to the horse for all the world as though he thought it would answer him. Solomon probably knew more about Tom than anyone else ever would, and James smiled to himself and guessed that he was now getting a full account of last night's meeting with Laura's pa.

He was about to relapse into day-dreams of Mary Ann again himself, when a commotion out in the yard startled him back to the present. Lookng outside, he saw a man desperately trying to keep his seat on a sweating, excitable horse and shouting for Mr Bates, who came running from his office.

"What's going on?" He stopped dead in his tracks as he recognised the man. "Oh, Mr Warner, sir. What's wrong?"

The man, gasping for breath and trying to hold his mount, still managed to bellow, "Get mounted man, quick. Mr Turner's had a terrible fall. We need help."

Mr Bates sprang into action. "Right, Tom help me saddle Solomon. Sam, take one of the others and ride to get Doctor Wellings."

Within minutes the stable yard was empty and the only sound to be heard was the rapidly retreating hoof-beats as the riders pounded away down the lane. After that, silence, which hung like an unseen blanket over all.

The stable lads looked at each other in mute dismay.

"W-we'd best carry on workin'," Tom said. "It won't do no good to stand around, worryin'." His face was dark with concern.

James went back to his work in the stall, but now his thoughts were firmly with Mr Turner and Sorrento.

Time dragged interminably. But after what seemed like hours, they heard the sound of a single horse approaching. Mr Bates rode into the yard alone and one look at his face was enough to tell them that it was not good news.

He dismounted and, as he stood holding the reins, his shoulders drooped and it was obvious that he was in some distress. He did not know how to begin what he had to say, and cleared his throat hard.

"I-I'm afraid the worst has happened. Mr Turner has been killed." There was a sharp intake of breath from the small crowd. Trying desperately to steady himself, Mr Bates continued, "I'm going up to the house to see Mrs Turner. Sam is helping Mr Warner take the ... take Mr Turner back there." He briefly lifted his head and James thought he saw the glitter of tears. "I'm afraid Sorrento has gone as well. Just carry on for now... If you can."

Then he re-mounted and turned Solomon to set off again, his back ramrod stiff.

Shock was mirrored in every face. It seemed impossible that on such a lovely sunny day, death had been so close at hand.

James felt his throat constricting, but he managed to call out. "Please, give Mrs Turner our respects." Mr Bates just nodded as he passed through the gateway.

Tom set off towards the little rest room. "Come on, we'd best brew a pot o' tea."

The men sat around holding their mugs, each deep in his own thoughts, all seemingly unable to talk. It was so sudden, so unreal. To lose one or the other would have been bad enough, but to lose both master and horse....

After a while, James wandered disconsolately back to Sorrento's stall. The straw gleamed golden, the hay lay in the small manger, soft and sweetly scented. It had been ready for his return, but now... The tears ran down his face in silent grief as utter disbelief battled with anger inside him.

He had liked and respected Mr Turner, both as a man and as a employer. He was a fair person, always ready to hear both sides of any argument—though James could never understand the preoccupation of the landed gentry to go hunting.

He pulled himself together, wiping the tears away on his sleeve, he wandered across the yard to where Tom was grooming Gretel. She was a lightly-built filly, kept for Mrs Turner or the children to ride. The pretty roan shook her head as Tom combed her mane, and the friends looked numbly at one another.

"Why, James, why both on 'em?" Tom asked.

But there was no answer, just a slow shake of the head. After a while, they began chatting desolately, each recalling happier times, each with his favourite story about the man they knew would never be replaced. Good employers were rare; so many estates were ruled by men who treated their staff—and sometimes their animals—with indifference and cruelty.

Later that day Mr Bates returned to the yard looking more composed, although still grim-faced, and called them all into his office.

"Mrs Turner is obviously very upset, but sends her thanks for your concern. She has no idea yet as to what she is going to do, so she has asked us to carry on as usual for now. The two young masters are abroad at the moment and she can't really make any decisions until they get home. As everything is in good order here I am letting you off early today. I think we all need time to get over the shock. Be on time tomorrow though—there'll be no slacking just because the master's not here, although I suppose I don't need to tell you that. I would just like you all to know that Mr Turner was well pleased with your work. He was very proud of his stables." He paused and swallowed hard. "Right, off you go." And he slumped back in his chair as the men filed out.

On reaching home James sat for a moment with his mother, before wandering out into the garden to sit on the log pile. Even after all these years he found it the place to bring him solace. His father found him still there when he arrived home a little later.

"Bad business, eh son?" He puffed on his pipe as James nodded.

"Why do they do it, pa?" His father knew what he meant. The hunting.

"Always done it, sort of tradition. Mr Turner ain't the first to die that way, yer know, an' won't be the last. Shame the 'orse 'ad to go an' all."

James blinked hard. "Don't know oo' I'll miss the most," he said.

John Newland wasn't surprised by his son's statement, knowing him as he did. "Wonder 'oo we'll get now. Can't see Mrs Turner keepin' the place on—she's always preferred bein' up in town, an' the sons ain't old enough yet." Then, with a sigh, "Ah well, I suppose we'd best get in fer tea, or yer ma'll be after us." He shook his head and tapped out his pipe. "It's a shame though, a real shame."

Chapter Six

But the day of Mr Turner's funeral found the Newland family reeling from another shock.

The estate staff had been granted a few hours leave and James arrived home in the afternoon to find his mother in such a state that he found it difficult to understand what she was trying to say.

Between sobs she told him, "Our Ellen, she's in gaol."

"W-what!" Surely his ears deceived him.

"The vicar came to see me, couple o' hours ago. What are we to do?"

"Ma, are yer sure you've got it right? There must be some mistake."

Ellen was one of James' older sisters. She had married a man called Robert Heath, from the nearby village of Farringdon, two years previously and went to live there with him on his parent's farm. Unfortunately, none of them had liked her husband. He had the reputation of being a drunkard and a bully and her parents had tried hard to dissuade her from marrying him, but to no avail. Although they had not seen much of her since her marriage, she had always appeared cheerful and in good health on her occasional visits.

Now James tried to comfort his mother. "Ma, don't fret, I'll go an' see vicar when pa gets 'ome. There must be a mistake, it'll be alright, just you see." He rubbed her shaking hands gently with his rough-skinned fingers, and prayed his father would arrive soon.

After what seemed like an eternity he heard his footsteps and, leaving his mother briefly, told him the news as he came through the door.

He too was stunned. "Seems unlikely for 'er to be in trouble, although she were a bit wayward in 'er younger days. Never did nothin' to get 'er in gaol though. Did 'e say which one she'd been taken to?" He looked at his wife ominously.

"Winchester." She looked up and their eyes locked. "She's in Winchester." It came out as a whisper.

There were a few moments silence before James moved. "Look, I'm goin' to see vicar. That a'right, pa? I shouldn't be long." His father nodded absently as James dashed out of the cottage and set off down the dusty street towards the vicarage.

His pace slowed as he approached the large and imposing grey-stone house. Meeting the vicar filled him with a considerable amount of anxiety as he had never spoken to him before, and even now he had no idea of what to say. Still, he thought, vicar or not, he was a man the same as any other.

Arriving at the solid door he banged hard with his fist, noticing too late the metal handle attached to a bell which hung to one side. He waited. Nothing. He was about to ring the bell when he heard, faintly, the sound of approaching footsteps from inside the house, and the door opened slowly to reveal a tiny sharp-featured woman.

"What do you want?" she asked. The voice matched the ice-pale eyes.

James swallowed hard and tried to modify his local dialect a little. "I'd like to see the vicar, if you please ma'am."

"Out of the question, we do not admit tramps here." She moved as though to slam the door in his face, but before she could, he spoke again.

"Please, I'm no tramp. I've come to see the reverend 'bout me sister. Me ma's worried sick." He held out a pleading hand "Please."

Her eyes narrowed as she weighed him up in her mind. "Wait there."

She closed the heavy door on him with surprising ease and he was left standing on the step to contemplate the state of his appearance. A tramp? He was just a typical village labourer dressed for work. But he'd been told that this vicar was a bit stuck up—a bit of a snob.

After what seemed a lifetime, he heard the sound of footsteps again and the woman opened the door once more. Did she look a little less stern? He couldn't be sure.

"If you've come on family business, the vicar will see you. This way." She ushered him along a dark, wood-panelled passage and into a small room at the end which smelt of beeswax.

There sat the vicar sat behind a large oak desk which almost dwarfed his skinny frame. He pointed to a chair, but James thought better of it, worried that his dirty clothes might spoil the material.

"Now, who is it you wish to see me about?" The man's pale grey eyes raked over him with something like disdain. So similar were they in appearance, that James thought that the vicar and the woman must be related.

He cleared his throat. "Please sir, I've come to enquire 'bout me sister Ellen—Ellen Heath, that is. Do yer know what's 'appened?" He held his breath.

"Ah, yes, Mrs Heath." The man tapped the side of his nose with a bony finger. "Sad business all round, sad business." Then looking James directly in the eye, "She has been accused of trying to poison her husband, Robert Heath. The complaint was brought by his mother, Mrs Elsie Heath, as he was deemed too ill at the time. Although he has now recovered, his wife—your sister—is awaiting trial in Winchester prison. Her case should be heard at the next assize session, which is on May the fourth." He coughed and looked down at his desk. "As she cannot afford legal representation," he lifted his hands dismissively, "things do not look too promising I'm afraid. It's a very serious charge." The cold eyes narrowed and he shook his head solemnly. "I think you should go home, comfort your mother and trust in God's good grace."

James stared, open-mouthed. "Er, is there nothin' else we can do? —Sir."

The vicar shook his head again and pursed his lips, obviously not wishing to discuss the matter further.

Mumbling his thanks for being seen, the young man left and walked sadly back out into the blinding afternoon sunshine.

How was he going to break this news to his parents? No easy way. But as he hurried homeward, although he had little idea of what to do next, he knew with a burning certainty that he must do something.

James arrived back at the cottage to find his father at work in the garden. He watched as John Newland thrust his garden fork vigorously into the soil time and again as though fighting some unseen demon, something more than just today's crisis, but at his son's approach he straightened his back and wiped the sweat from his brow with a bare arm.

"What did yer find out son?"

"Sorry pa, the vicar couldn't tell me much. Nothin' to 'elp Ellen. 'E didn't seem all that bothered, to be 'onest." James pulled a long face. "What can we do?"

The question hung between them in the still air as a bee buzzed from one pale rose to another in the nearby hedge. With a loud sigh, the older man turned and walked into the cottage, and in the tiny kitchen he went to stand at his wife's side.

"It's no use mother, vicar can't 'elp."

"'Ow can this 'ave 'appened? It don't seem right." Ann Newland wept.

James had followed his father indoors, but his parents' pain was more than he could bear. "I'm goin' to Farringdon tomorrer," he announced.

Two pairs of eyes turned on him, and his father put up a hand. "Now, just yer 'old on a minute. Yer can't go trampin' all over the place just like that. Lets sleep on it." He took his wife's hand in his again, but it was little comfort to the woman and her tears continued unchecked.

But James had made up his mind. Even if he had to go alone, go he would.

His mother pleaded with him the next morning to wait. "Arthur or William will go with yer, if y'll just be patient. Them 'Eath's ain't known for their friendliness at best o' times."

He patted her shoulder. "It'll be a'right, ma. I'll be fine." The confidence in his voice belied the churning in his stomach. He had to get time off from work before he could do anything, and facing Mr Bates bore more fear for him than all the Heath family put together.

He arrived at the yard early, hoping to catch the manager before work began for the day, but the only person around was a bleary-eyed night-watchman, none too pleased at having been caught emerging from the rest-room, blanket in hand.

Then to James' relief, Tom appeared, his face alight with merriment as usual. "'Ello mate, you're early." He peered closer, "Cor, yer look terrible, what's wrong?"

James told his friend the tale of his sister's arrest, and as he did so Tom's eyes filled with genuine concern. "Bloody 'ell, what a thing to 'appen. You 'opin' old Bates'll lend yer an 'orse?"

James nodded.

"'Ere 'e is now, go an' see 'im." Tom gave him a nudge with his elbow. "Good luck," he whispered.

James was tense as he strode towards the office. He gulped hard, drew a deep breath and explained the situation to Mr Bates as best he could. The man's behaviour did not help the situation, as he continued to shuffle papers around his desk and, at times, appeared to be hardly listening.

His story finished, James held his breath, waiting for an answer.

Mr Bates studied him for several minutes, obviously struggling with something inside himself.

Then, "No, I can't let you go in working hours. Your family's business is just that, and none of mine. We are not going to let standards drop just because Mr Turner is no longer here. These stables will be fully manned at all times. Now, back to work, you have plenty to do—and so have I."

Tears threatened, but James gritted his teeth and turned disconsolately away, stepping out into the grey, drizzle-damp yard.

He hurried over to the tack room, where he knew Tom would be waiting.

"I can see it's not good news," his friend said after a glance at his glum face. "Never mind, yer can go straight after work." But he knew that patience was not one of James' virtues.

Heavy-hearted, James went to muck out Gretel's stall. The young horse nuzzled him and whinnied softly, bringing a fleeting smile to his lips. Burying his face in her mane, he moaned, "Oh, what shall I do..."

The door rattled behind him. "'Ere, stop making love to that 'orse, an' listen."

James grinned—Tom never failed to cheer him up, no matter what happened. "What do yer want?" he asked.

His friend grinned wickedly. "Ol' Bates 'as gone out. Goin' t' be gone most o' the day, accordin' to Fred. Now's yer chance to get off. We'll cover for yer if Sam asks where yer are."

James bit his lip, "D' yer think I dare?" He stood for a moment, undecided, not wanting to get the others into trouble.

"Yeh, go on." Tom urged.

James moved towards the door. "Right, but I'll walk—I'm not riskin' takin' an 'orse. Thanks mate."

Making sure that Sam was nowhere to be seen, he hurried across the yard, out of the gates, and set off at a fair pace along the road to Farringdon about three miles away.

The narrow and twisting lane with high, hedge-topped banks, sheltered him from the light rain. Away to the west though, the sky was clearing, bringing hope of fine weather later on in the day.

The fresh air and sense of freedom made him feel better and he started to enjoy the walk, suddenly noticing that the hedgerows were alive with new growth. Clusters of primroses turned their faces up to where the sun should be and a few wild daffodils nodded gently, as if enjoying some private conversation. His progress disturbed the nesting birds and they flew in and out of the trees, chirruping a loud warning. This was just how it used to be, when he was a boy, and he called softly to a blackbird, delighting in its answering song. He could not help thinking how much simpler life had been then.

His step became more purposeful. No time for reminiscing—he was a man now and had to do manly things, but he was overjoyed as the sun suddenly found a break in the cloud. The shaft of brilliance brought out the colours of the blossom and the many hues of green bursting forth amongst the tree-tops.

His spirits lifted. Life never seemed so bad when the sun was shining.

Soon he could see the tower of Farringdon church peeping through the greenery and beside it the dark form of a large Yew tree, very like the one in his own village. He could not help wishing he were back there now.

Then he realised that he did not know exactly where the Heath's farm was. Perhaps he could find someone to point him in the right direction. But the village appeared deserted, with an air of disquiet which seemed almost tangible.

James shook himself—now he was being fanciful. But truth be told, some of the cottages did look rather unkempt, and others almost derelict.

His footsteps echoed along the dusty road, the nails in his boots clawing the surface. He slowed his pace, his heart beat loud in his own ears. How was he ever to find his way? He realised now that he should have waited for one of his brothers to accompany him.

Then, just when he was thinking of turning back, he saw two women ahead of him along the street. They had emerged from a small shop at the corner of a crossroads, deep in conversation.

He hurried up and addressed them politely. "Excuse me, could yer tell me where the Heath family live ... please?"

The women shot a look at each other and then back at him.

"What do you want with the likes o' them, then?" one said sharply, while the other nodded.

"Er, well, I—I 'ave to see 'em. It's important," James shifted his feet uncomfortably.

"Best to keep away, I'd say. Still if you 'ave to see 'em..." The woman hesitated. She obviously wanted to know what this was all about, but James was unforthcoming.

She sighed. "Go straight on along the street then," she pointed, "and 'bout half a mile further on you'll see a turnin'. It's up there, not far, but you'll smell it first anyway." She threw a knowing look at her companion and they hurried off in the direction from which James had just come.

How curious, he thought to himself. They had been almost hostile. Seemed as if the Heath family were not much liked hereabouts. His father's words of caution to Ellen when she had announced her intention of marrying into it rang suddenly in James ears, and he set off once more with anxiety gnawing at his insides.

The cottages gave way abruptly to open countryside, the road flanked by high hedges and wide muddy ditches. The young man frowned, had he missed the turning? But then ahead he saw a break in the hawthorn hedge.

At first he was convinced that no one could be living here, for at the end of it stood a derelict farmhouse, but then he noticed a thin plume of smoke rising from the chimney stack. Where the windows should have been there were just open spaces, tiles were missing from the roof, and outside the doorway, in among a few scrawny hens, stood a herd of about twenty even scrawnier cows.

James was stunned. His own home was poor, but this … this was a hovel. Surely Ellen could not have lived here.

He forced himself to walk towards the house. There, where the cows and fowl vied for the same patch of muddy ground, sat a small child.

James' tentative, "'Ello," was greeted with a blank stare, as the child ignored him and carried on playing, digging a stick into the glutinous mud. And there was plenty of it around. Never had he seen so much mess, even in a farmyard. The smell was appalling, the worst he had ever come across.

But the child…

"Is anyone around?" James asked the youngster, who seemed to be about two years old—too young to be out here on its own, he was sure.

Another blank stare.

James sighed and turned his attention to the door. It stood ajar, hanging drunkenly off its top hinge. He knocked tentatively on the blistered wood.

No answer. He knocked again, louder. Surely someone was here, the child could not be on its own.

"Yeh! 'oo is it?" A raucous voice came from inside, then a woman appeared the like of whom James had never seen before in all his life.

She was enormous, several chins hanging down to join the ample flesh of her breasts. A large head was sparsely covered with frizzy red hair, on top of which sat a cloth cap. Hostile blue eyes glared at him, red cheeks puffed out, rancid breath issuing from between black stumps of teeth. Her clothes were filthy.

James was speechless. It took every scrap of courage he possessed to ask, "Are yer Mrs Heath?" He longed for her to say, no.

"What if I am, 'Oo wants t' know?" She spat.

He recoiled, as much from the stench as fear.

"M-me name's James Newland. Ellen's brother. I want to know … what 'appened."

At the sound of the girl's name, Mrs Heath flew into a fury. "What 'appened? What 'appened?" she shrieked, "I'll tell yer what 'appened. She tried to kill my son. Put poison in 'is dinner she did, makin' out they was mushrooms, evil bitch. Nothin' but trouble, ever since she came. Whinin' an' wimperin', never a proper wife to poor Rob. Never doin' 'er bit to 'elp." She ranted on. "Knew she'd be trouble, warned 'im, I did. Don't know why 'e married 'er, she ain't even pretty, 'er nor 'er brat. Well, she's gone now an' good riddance, I say. So clear off. Go on, back t' yer trouble-makin' family. Bad lot thru' an' thru' the lot o' y'are."

The words were spat out, spraying James with the woman's spittle, causing him to step back so quickly that he nearly fell over in the mud.

"Go on, clear orf, else I'll get me 'usband on to yer" She shook her fist at him, leaving James in no doubt that she would strike him herself if he did not move. He did not need telling twice. With his head whirling from the onslaught, he beat a hasty retreat, and on reaching the safety of the lane, he stopped and looked back. The woman was nowhere to be seen … but the child still played on in the mud.

The homeward journey held no pleasure for him. His thoughts were all with his sister. Whatever Ellen was supposed to have done, he was sure that she did not deserve such treatment. How could she have lived in that place? The thought kept going round and round in his head. How?

Something else the woman had said pushed its way into James' mind. "'Er brat," she'd said. A child, Ellen has a child. Oh, dear God, how was he going to tell his mother. She would be broken-hearted. A grandchild—a small baby she had known nothing about—and now he guessed in prison with its mother. How could they do such a thing, the Heath family? How could they? And, where was Robert Heath—didn't he care about his child? There were many unanswered questions going around in James' mind. Not least, the accusation that the whole family were trouble-makers.

Mrs Heath had been a thoroughly unpleasant person—perhaps she had invented things to cover for her son. That thought had to comfort him as he made his way back to Selborne.

Arriving back at the stables, luck was on his side for once. Mr Bates was still away, and he found his workmates in the tack room working quietly. Tom hurried across to grab him by the arm as he entered.

"Yer look all in mate, come an' sit down," he said, and led him towards a bale of straw. "Tell us what 'appened."

James looked in despair from one to another. Where could he start? Taking a deep breath, he launched into his tale, telling as best he could, about the Heath family home, and what had happened there, finishing with, "'Onest, I'm not makin' it up, it really were that bad."

"Cor, it's 'ard to believe, ain't it?" Tom shook his head in disbelief.

And James could only agree.

He was not sure how he got through the rest of the afternoon. He wanted the day to end, and yet he was not looking forward to returning home that evening. When he did, he found his mother scrubbing furiously at the kitchen floor. Tears streamed down her face to drop and mingle with the soap-suds on the flagstones.

"Ma?" He rushed to her side and pulled her gently to her feet. "What are yer doin' that for, at this time o' day?" The floor usually had its daily wash after the menfolk had left for work.

Ann Newland ran her hand across a red perspiring face. "I dropped the chicken mash. Just went out of me 'ands. Oh, yer should 'ave seen the mess." She tried a weak smile. "I don't know what's wrong with me, really I don't."

James put a comforting arm around his mother's shoulders. "Yer worryin' yerself sick 'bout Ellen, that's what's wrong. Come an' sit down an' I'll make yer a cup o' tea."

In spite of herself his mother laughed. "What! Since when did yer know 'ow to brew tea?"

He feigned a wounded look. "I do it all the time at work. Well, once a week, we take it in turns. At least it made yer smile."

"Oh, you," his mother chuckled again and waved a hand towards him. "Go on then, let's see yer."

Ten minutes later when John Newland walked through the door, he thought he had come to the wrong house. There was his youngest son standing at the stove, pouring boiling water into a teapot.

"'Ello dear," his wife said, "look, we've got a manservant."

"So I see," John said. "Bit scruffy though, ain't 'e?"

"Ma were upset so I thought it were the least I could do."

John looked at her, "What were yer upset about then, mother?"

She explained, looking somewhat shamefaced. Her husband shook his head and said much the same as his son had done.

James placed the mugs of tea on the table and sat down next to his mother, motioning his father to join them.

Leaving out some of the more gruesome details, he told them of his visit to Farringdon. John drew in his breath sharply. "I told yer to wait. Why d'yer 'ave t' be so impatient?" he sighed.

"My poor Ellen. Why did she put up with living like that, she could 'ave come 'ome. An' 'er 'avin' a babe," Ann Newland shook her head and looked at her husband, "Why didn't she tell us, John, why?"

"I don't know dear. Must 'ave 'ad her reasons I 'spose, tho' goodness knows what they could 'ave bin." He sat, shoulders drooped, and James couldn't help noticing how old he had begun to look over the past few days.

Then suddenly he straightened his shoulders and declared, "I'm goin' to Winchester."

"No, John. You can't, even for Ellen. Yer too old to go traipsing all over the countryside."

But James nearly jumped off his seat, looking ready to be off there and then. "I'll come with yer, pa. We'll be alright, ma."

His father held up a cautioning hand. "Hold on, hold on. I'm goin' to ask Arthur to come with me." Then, as James tried to butt in, "Don't argue, son. I want yer 'ere to keep an eye on yer ma—she'll need a man around." And with that James had to be content.

"When are yer goin', John?" his wife asked.

"Depends when Arthur can get time off, but soon. I'll ask me foreman tomorrer if it's alright."

"'Ow are yer goin', pa. Yer ain't goin' to walk, are yer?" James thought that at the age of fifty-eight his father was too old to walk the distance.

55

"'Course we are. We'll take it steady. I'm not passed it yet yer know," his father grinned. "It's only about twenty-five miles or so anyway, not hundreds." He looked at his wife, "eh, mother?"

James was puzzled at the glance one gave the other. His mother noticed and told him gently with a smile, "We'll explain it to yer one day, son."

The memory of something that Mrs Heath had said came into James mind then. "What did that woman mean 'bout us bein' trouble-makers. We ain't, are we, pa?"

"No son, pay no mind to 'er. Can't think what she were on about." But he threw his wife another knowing look, and it did not go unnoticed by their son either.

His father eased himself from the wooden bench. "I'd best dig a few vegetables for the pot."

"An' I'd best get us some dinner," replied Ann Newland going to busy herself at the stove.

And their youngest son was left to wonder what mystery it was that his parents were hiding from him.

56

Chapter Seven

As he pushed open the gate at Honeysuckle Cottage, James could see Mr Butler in the porchway, dozing in his old wickerwork armchair. He was almost hidden from view by a swathe of blankets, but his face peered out from the folds and broke into a wide smile at the sight of his young friend.

"'Ello there, James lad. 'Ow be you today? Come to chop a bit o' wood for us, 'ave yer?"

"'Ello, Mr Butler. No, not t'day—I've just come to see 'ow y'are." He gazed at the old man and tried to hide his worry. The once robust and energetic man had become a shadow of his former self, and James knew that Mrs Butler was concerned about him.

"Not so bad, son. Me leg's is playin' me up a bit, that's all." He gave a gap-toothed smile.

James sat down on the stone step at the man's feet. "Can I ask yer somethin ... somethin' 'bout me family?"

"Yer lookin' worried lad, what's wrong?"

The young man took a deep breath and plunged into the tale of Ellen and his recent visit to Farringdon—leaving out some of the worst parts just as he had with his parents.

Mr Butler shook his head and tut-tutted from time to time.

"So what I want to know," said James eventually, "is why did Mrs Heath say we was trouble makers?"

Mr Butler studied him keenly and pursed his lips. "'Tisn't my place to go tellin' tales. Won't yer pa tell yer?"

James shook his head. "He an' me ma are so worried 'bout Ellen, I didn't like to press 'em. 'E did try to laugh it off, but I know they was 'idin' somethin'."

"Well..." the old man paused, "I'll tell yer what I know. It ain't much mind, 'cos I was workin' away at the time and only 'eard 'bout it later on."

James waited as patiently as he could, while Mr Butler sat deep in thought with one spidery finger rubbing his chin.

Then he cleared his throat and took a deep breath. "It were a couple o' years afor you were born. There were a lot o' village folk here in Selborne—and in some other places as well I think—who were very angry 'cos the vicar wanted his tithes to stay at the same

57

rate, which weren't fair 'cos there 'adn't been no decent weather for so long that the crops 'ad failed. That meant the farmers 'ad very little to sell, so wages was almost nothin' an' the labourers' families was starvin'." He drew another breath, "Anyway, apparently one evenin' in the pub, some o' the menfolk got talkin' an decided they'd 'ave to sort somethin' out. They couldn't afford to buy so much as a loaf of bread—they was all livin' on next to nothin' an' the price o' bread kept goin' up." He paused again, gazing off into space, as though to see more clearly back over the years.

"If I remember rightly, it were decided that someone should go to the vicar an' see if 'e would reduce the tithe so as the workers could be paid enough to live on." Mr Butler shook his head, "Don't know 'ow folk survived, that I don't. That was why I went to work in Winchester, yer know. Well, in the end, several men went to see 'im—Reverend Cobbold 'twer then—but 'e wouldn't budge. Told 'em 'e couldn't afford to reduce the money paid to 'im. 'Is attitude made the men mad. It were alright for 'im—'e 'ad plenty, but 'e didn't care 'bout the villagers scrapin' a livin'."

He stopped and closed his eyes, and James wondered if he had gone to sleep, feeling a little guilty at having tired him out, but suddenly the old man's eyes opened and he carried on. "Then, the men 'ears 'as 'ow the same thing 'ad 'appened somewhere else and when they'd threatened the vicar there, 'e 'ad done what 'e were asked. 'Course, this gave some o' the men 'ere an idea, an' they decided to get together an' go to 'im in a mob. They thought that p'raps they could make 'im play fair." He chuckled, "I wish I'd been 'ere. I'd 'ave joined 'em, y'know." He sat quietly reflecting again for several minutes.

James' mind raced. What part had his father played in all this? The event had obviously been important, otherwise it would not have been so well remembered by Mr Butler. He wondered why he had never heard about it before and whether his older brothers and sisters knew. He was anxious to hear more and fidgeted, but Mr Butler seemed to be resting.

After a few moments, the old man roused himself again. "Sorry 'bout that son. I get tired so quickly now."

"Are yer sure yer want to carry on? I can come another day to 'ear the rest." James held his breath, torn between wanting to hear more of the story and not wanting to tire Mr Butler.

"I'll be alright, lad. Now, where did I get to? Ah, yes. Y'see some of the trouble was that the men always 'eld their meetings in the pub, so sometimes the ale did the talkin', if yer know what I mean." He gave a wheezy laugh, which made him cough and he had to pause to get his breath back. "Yer pa weren't involved at that time, but yer ma 'eard 'bout what the men were planning an' decided to tell Mrs Cobbold. Not that the reverend took any notice—'e thought 'imself above other folk. 'Course, word soon spread 'bout the meetin' an' it weren't just the labourers 'oo was involved either. The tradesmen an' farmers were behind them, 'cos they was nearly as bad off themselves." He smiled, "Not many people livin' 'ere abouts was able to eat every day y'know."

James stared. "No, I never realised." Then he remembered the conversation he'd had one day many years ago with his father. So many things became clearer. The tiny kitchen hung around with wet washing, the meagre meals, and all the mending and making do with clothes and shoes. He felt guilty now when he remembered the many occasions when he had arrived home with clothes dirty and torn, and his boots caked in mud. How his mother must have dreaded him coming through the door.

But, Mr Butler was speaking again. "You're wonderin' where yer pa comes into all this ain't yer?

James nodded slowly.

"Well, I 'eard it 'appened like this. When the men was decidin' what to do, they thought as 'ow it would be a good idea to 'ave someone to act as a leader. As yer know yer pa 'as 'is trumpet from the war, so 'e was chosen, an' when the crowd gathered early in the mornin' outside the vicarage, 'e was there, blowin' 'is 'orn to call all the men together." Mr Butler chuckled. "I wish I'd been 'ere. They called the vicar out of 'is bed, an' 'e came to see 'em, but 'e wouldn't change 'is tune. 'E were stubborn, that one. They tried everythin' to make 'im see sense, even makin' threats against him an' 'is family. It did no good, so they gave 'im 'alf-an-hour to think on it. Trouble was," He scratched his nose and sucked in his breath. "The crowd got out of 'and an' for some unknown reason a few 'undred marched down the road to the work'ouse. Bad business that were, ransacked the place they did. Frightened the family o' the man 'oo ran it an' chucked all their belongings out, started fires… Oh, it must 'ave been terrible. Some'ow yer pa an' a few of the others saw sense. They didn't want to see another man's 'ome destroyed, so they called the mob off. Trouble was by the time they got back to the vicarage, they was bayin' for blood." He pulled the blankets tighter around himself as the evening air began to lose its warmth. "Mind you, the vicar must 'ave thought things through—whether it were fear of the mob or not, no one knows, but 'e agreed to sign the paper to reduce the payments. Fair broke 'is 'eart, so I was told."

James sat quietly for a moment and noticed that Mr Butler had dozed off, his pale lips quivering at each breath. It was such a shame to see the old man like this, but he was glad that he'd asked about pa, otherwise he may never have known. Now he'd have to get his side of the story too—he must know the whole truth. He wondered if that was the reason for his father's objection to ale. Mr Butler had mentioned the ale doing the talking—perhaps that was how he had got involved.

A slight movement from within the blanket caught his attention.

"Are yer alright, Mr Butler. Do yer want to go inside?"

"Not yet, son—you've not 'eard the worst yet."

James eyes opened wide. What else could there be? "If yer sure yer can go on, then I'm listenin'," he said.

"Well, no one knows for sure why, but the followin' day the mob all set off for the next village. Once they got there, things got really ugly an' they almost demolished the work'ouse there too—goodness knows what they thought they was doin'. Don't know if yer pa were there that day—you'll 'ave to asked 'im yerself 'bout that."

"I'm going to—he'll have to tell me all about it now, won't he?"

"Mmm. Trouble was, yer see, the military was called in an' they went an' rounded up all them involved in the two days rioting, yer pa amongst 'em. 'E got sent to Winchester prison for six months." Mr Butler looked at the stunned face. "'E were luckier than most though. You can wonder what was lucky 'bout gaol, but many of the men got sent to prison ships and transported to the other side of the world. They never came back."

"But pa wasn't sent with them?"

"No. 'Is boss spoke up for 'im, an' once it were realised that 'e didn't actually organise the trouble-makers they decided to let 'im off lightly. So 'e wasn't sent."

"It must 'ave been 'ard on the families of them that were. Even 'arder than before I 'spose."

"Yes it was—an' that's why some folk are against yer pa. They thought 'e should 'ave gone as well. I'm afraid our Charlotte is one of 'em. She was goin' to marry one o' those men and she's been bitter ever since."

Suddenly, Mrs Butler peered around the door. "You two stayin' out 'ere all night?" she asked. But she was smiling.

Her husband roused himself at the sound of her voice. "We'd better be comin' in, I 'spose. It's gettin' late right enough. 'Elp me up, James lad."

Between them Mrs Butler and James got the elderly man into his armchair indoors beside the fire and Mrs Butler gave him his nightcap of a tot of rum. "For me chest." He explained.

James was puzzled. Why was Charlotte Knight bitter about her young man being sent away? Surely, Mary Ann had been born since then... But he would have to ask about that another time, as it was clear that Mr Butler was completely exhausted tonight.

He made his excuses to leave, and set off for home up the lane, his mind buzzing with unanswered questions. He would have to pester his parents until he was told the whole story. But perhaps he had better wait until the problem of Ellen was sorted out. At the moment, John and Ann Newland had more than enough on their plate ... and not for the first time by all accounts.

Chapter Eight

The following morning James waited impatiently for a chance to speak to his friend, and when at last they were alone in the tack room Tom grinned and said, "What is it? You're fair burstin' to tell me somethin'."

James frowned, was he really so transparent? But quickly he related some of what Mr Butler had told him the night before, and to his amazement, Tom just nodded.

"Yeh, I knew about that. I were a baby at the time o' course, but me ma an' pa talked of it sometimes. They'd only just moved to Selborne, so my pa didn't get involved. I remember when you first come to work 'ere, 'im saying yer pa were one of those there. Sorry, didn't know you knew nothin' 'bout it." He paused to fasten a buckle to the leather head band that he had been cleaning.

James mumbled an answer, mortified to think that Tom, and probably everyone else in the village, knew something that he didn't. He was just about to add that he was proud of his father, when there was a commotion outside in the yard.

They ran across to the door to be met by an irate Mr Bates. Close on his heels were Fred and Joe, who were pulling faces behind his back.

"Right, now I've got the whole lazy bunch of you together, just listen. This place is a disgrace, look at it."

They all looked at the neat and tidy stable yard, and then back at Mr Bates.

"Get it cleaned up. I want it spotless. Do you here?" He bellowed. "We've a man called Wytherley-Jones, a prospective buyer, coming to view the place in half-an-hour. He's seen the rest of the estate and I don't want this place to put him off. Now, jump to it." With that he stalked off to his office.

The four men looked at each other for barely a second. Understanding that this man must be of some importance, they dashed off in different directions to clean and scrub what was already as perfect as could be.

Tom gave vent to his feelings once he and James were in the safe confines of the loose boxes. "Bloomin' cheek. Wish I could give 'im a piece o' me mind sometimes. Still, this bloke must be keen to buy the estate, so best keep on 'is good side I 'spose, otherwise we'll be out o' our jobs."

Half an hour later, Mr Bates called them all into the yard. With him was a man to whom James took an instant dislike. He could not think why, although perhaps it was the way he looked down his nose at everyone, even Mr Bates.

Mr Wytherley-Jones was short, stocky, and loud. His florid cheeks and frizzy hair rather reminded James of Mrs Heath, and he had to struggle hard at first to control his mirth.

The inspection began, with the man poking his large head into every nook and cranny, the stalls and tack-room, even the hay-loft. Mr Bates walked behind, hands clasped behind his back, knuckles white from barely-concealed anger. He knew only too well that the stables were immaculate, although Mr Wytherley-Jones seemed intent on finding fault.

Once the inspection was over, the would-be owner stood in the middle of the yard and looked at the men lined up before him, then turned to Mr Bates and said in his strident voice, "I like what I see so far. The horses could do with a more thorough grooming, of course and there are one or two areas that need attention, but on the whole..." And he tapped the side of his leather-clad leg with the riding crop he was carrying and puffed out his chest.

James was standing next to Tom and felt his body shake with an anger which matched his own. How dare this man come here and say such things. Mr Turner had always been pleased with the way things were, and the men had kept up the same standards even now he was no longer there.

Mr Wytherley-Jones turned to Mr Bates and declared that he had seen enough for today, but might want to come again, probably one day the following week. Then he turned and walked, as swiftly as his bulk would allow, to the waiting buggy. This dipped alarmingly as he climbed aboard and the poor horse scrabbled for a foot-hold at the feel of the whip.

Mr Bates returned, even more grim-faced, to his office.

"Well," Tom exploded, once the men were in their own rest-room, "I'm lost for words, 'onest I am. What a nasty piece o' work 'e is. I can't see me gettin' on with 'im, never."

The others agreed. Not one of them had anything good to say about the man.

"Let's 'ope 'e don't buy the place, that's all." James said. "It would be awful. An' did yer see the way 'e whipped 'is 'orse?"

"Don't reckon 'e knows anythin' 'bout runnin' stables, if yer ask me. That talk were all for show," said Fred. The others nodded and sat in gloomy silence, their mugs of tea untouched.

Later, at home, John Newland told of similar scenes at both the cow-sheds and the dairy earlier in the day. The future did not look too rosy for the workers on Home Farm estate.

Very early on the Monday morning following Mr Wytherley-Jones' visit to the stables, James and his mother watched John Newland and his son Arthur set off down the lane to start their long walk to Winchester.

It was a misty morning, but there was the promise of a warm, sunny day to come and James wished with all his heart that he was going too.

The men had very little to carry and hardly any money between them. The hope was that they would be offered refreshment from kind cottagers along the way.

John's idea was to hang on to the seven pennies in his purse, in case a bribe might effect a meeting with his daughter. His wife had given them enough bread and cheese to last the first day, but was fretting about them not getting anything else. Their bedding consisted of one sack each, which would help in some small way to keep the worst of the night's chill off.

It was an emotional parting, and once the men were out of sight James and his mother wandered back into the cottage. It was filled with the smell of baking bread, and Ann Newland hurried over to the stove, lifted the oven door open with the hem of her apron and removed two loaves. The bread taken by her husband and son meant a fresh supply had to be made, much to James' delight. He enjoyed nothing better for his breakfast than a hunk of fresh-baked home-made bread, spread with butter and topped off with a good helping of Mrs Butler's crab-apple jelly.

"That's the last o' the flour 'til the weekend, so don't go stuffin' yerself." His mother warned.

James grinned at her. "As if I would." Then he put an arm around her shoulders. "Don't worry too much 'bout 'em ma, they can look after 'emselves."

"I know," she smiled weakly. "I just 'ope they can get to see Ellen, an' 'er baby. Poor little mite. 'Oo could do such a thing?" She sighed and turned the bread from the tins to cool on the scrubbed wooden table.

Eliza and Harriet appeared at that moment, ready to grab a bite to eat and then be on their way to the dairy where they both worked. They chatted on about Ellen and her baby daughter, until their mother bade them be quiet. It was just too upsetting for her, and James wondered at his sisters' stupidity. Couldn't they see how it was affecting their mother? He just hoped that there would be better news when his father and Arthur returned later in the week.

When he arrived back home after work that day, James was surprised to find Mrs Butler sitting in the kitchen with his mother. In all the years that the two families had been friends he could not recall either Mr or Mrs Butler visiting his home. The elderly woman sat now, ashen faced, in the wooden armchair, and James feared the worst.

His mother looked up at him. "I'm afraid Mr Butler passed away this morning."

He stood mute for a moment as the news sunk in.

Mrs Butler nodded, tears welling, "It was sudden, but peaceful. 'E just went off to sleep in his chair, an' when I went to see if 'e wanted a cup o' tea, 'e'd gone." She sniffed and dabbed her eyes with a large white handkerchief. "I don't know what I'll do now, I feel so lost. Nearly fifty years we'd been wed," she shook her head sadly. "Nearly fifty years."

James went over to her, bent down and took one of her soft hands in his. "I'm so sorry, really I am." He blinked back the threatening tears. "It's 'ard to think I were with 'im a couple o' days ago. I was that fond of 'im, 'e were almost like a grandad to me. An' so good an' kind...."

This made Mrs Butler cry even more, but she patted him on the shoulder. "He was very fond o' you too. You've 'elped us a lot over years, an' I know 'e appreciated everything. Me an' all, I'll never be able to thank you enough."

Then wiping the tears away she said, "Well, I must be gettin' back 'ome, Charlotte an' Mary Ann should be 'ere soon. Verger offered to pick 'em up when I was at the vicarage seein' 'bout the funeral." This brought on another spasm of weeping, but she composed herself enough to say, "The funeral's on Thursday afternoon, I 'ope you can both come. Bye for now."

After she'd gone, James turned to his mother. "It were a bit sudden, weren't it ma?"

She smiled knowingly at her son. "Not really. 'E'd been getting frailer by the month. Somethin' in 'is insides weren't right, I should think. Will yer be able to get time off work for the funeral?"

"Dunno. Old Bates is in a stew 'bout the new man, but I'll try. I would like to go, it wouldn't seem right not to." Then it struck him—Mary Ann would be there. In spite of the situation, it would be lovely to see her. But the thought made him feel guilty.

On Tuesday morning, Mr Bates called the men together to inform them that Mr Wytherley-Jones was now the new owner of Home Farm estate—and an ill-concealed groan went round.

"That'll do. 'E's our employer now, so lets make the best of it. By the way, he is bringing his son here tomorrow morning to pick up horses and go riding. I'll decide who to get saddled-up later on. Right, back to work now." Even Mr Bates did not seem too thrilled with the situation, although he would never have admitted it.

As Mr Wytherley-Jones' own horses had not yet arrived, it meant that he would need two of the resident ones, and as James said to Tom, "I ain't too keen on 'im ridin' any o' our'n."

For once, Mr Bates was undecided and kept changing his mind as to which horses to saddle. No one knew how old the younger Wytherley-Jones was, but it was reckoned that he could not be any more than in his early teens. In the end it was decided to get Blackie, a big strong hunter, ready for the father and for his son, Gretel, the pretty bay.

When at last the two entered the yard, there was a deathly hush. If the stable staff had disliked the father on sight, then they positively hated the son. Godfrey was a larger, and if possible more aggressive, version of his father.

The same complexion, large head and hard, granite-coloured eyes and cruel mouth all mirrored the older man. He even swaggered into the yard copying his father's habit of tapping his whip against leather gaiters.

The thought of him riding gentle Gretel sent shivers down James' back and he guessed the others felt the same.

Mr Bates was lost for words, but managed to splutter, "Oh, I'm sorry, sir. I had no idea your young son was so old—I mean, er…"

Then Tom stepped forward. "I'll saddle a bigger mount for yer, sir," he said, tugging his forelock. "We thought as 'ow Master Wytherley-Jones was a little lad, beggin' yer pardon sir."

"Yes," Mr Bates, regained his composure, throwing a thankful glance at Tom. "We didn't think you were old enough to have a grown-up son."

James grinned, what a load of flannel, but none the less true, if he was honest.

Mr Wytherley-Jones waved his hand impatiently. "No need for all this fuss. Godfrey can manage perfectly well. Come on boy, let's get off."

Mr Bates tried to dissuade him, but was given a glare venomous enough to silence even the most stout-hearted and, to the dismay of all, the two men went riding out of the yard with Godfrey Wytherley-Jones looking ridiculous astride the small horse.

"I 'ope 'e don't ride 'er too 'ard," Tom said, "she ain't used to it. Mr Turner kept 'er for the ladies to use."

James nodded. "'Ard lookin' sod, an' all."

They were surprised when Mr Bates voiced his concern as well. He had never passed an opinion on anything in front of his staff before, but he was obviously worried too. At last he told them, "Back to work now, there's nothing we can do." But it was said quietly, most unlike his usual brusque tongue.

The men returned to their chores. They had been clearing some of the unused stalls in readiness for the arrival of the new owner's horses. James had the task of white-washing the stall that had once housed Sorrento. It had not been used since his death as no one, not even Mr Bates, had the heart to put another animal in there.

He continued wielding the long-handled brush to coat the walls with the sloshy liquid—getting almost as much on himself as anywhere else. As he worked his thoughts turned to Mr Butler and all the good times he had spent in the old man's company. It would seem strange not having him there to tell his troubles to or, as the other evening, someone to tell him tales of the past.

Oblivious to his spattered appearance, he worked steadily on, his thoughts moving to his father and brother. They should be in Winchester now, had they managed to see Ellen yet?

Suddenly, he was brought back to the present by the clatter of hooves on cobbles, and Tom's voice, unusually loud.

He crossed to the doorway to see what was going on and the sight which met his eyes would stay with him forever.

Tom was standing in the middle of the yard, fists clenched and his face furious as he stood up to Godfrey Wytherley-Jones.

The reason was only too apparent.

67

One look at Gretel told its own story. Blood from her torn and bleeding mouth dripped onto the ground beneath foam-specked legs and she was heaving to draw breath through flaring nostrils, obviously in a severely distressed state.

Mr Bates was trying, unsuccessfully, to pull Tom away, although even he must have been appalled at the state of the horse.

Godfrey's father sat passively in his saddle, even a hint of amusement playing at the corners of his mouth.

Tom was completely beside himself with anger. "Look at 'er? Yer wicked bugger yer. Yer've nearly killed 'er. What did yer think yer was doin'? Don't yer know 'ow to treat an' 'orse proper?" The tirade seemed to go on and on, with Godfrey's sneering face making the matter worse.

He stepped closer and thrust his face into Tom's. "Don't you dare to speak to me like that. Who do you think you are? Nothing but common scum. I'll treat my horse any way I think fit, it's nothing to do with you. Now get out of my way." He raised his whip threateningly.

But Tom had not finished. "I may be common, but I know 'ow to treat animals, I don't go round 'urtin' 'em." He shook off another attempt to pull him away by Mr Bates. "Look at 'er, an' 'er such a gentle creature." He was nearly in tears by now. "Come on Gretel old girl, let's sort yer out." He reached forward to take the horses reins.

But Godfrey would have none of that. "Just you apologise, boy," the last word spat out. "You're not going to speak to me like that and get away with it. Apologise, do you hear me? Now. And keep away from that horse, she's only fit for the knacker's yard, anyway."

Tom's mouth dropped open and his already dark eyes turned to black as he struggled to keep his hands to himself. "Yer evil, yer are, evil." He snarled.

The two men glared at each other, face's barely more a few inches apart, pure hatred emanating from both.

James watched the tableau in shocked silence. He had never seen Tom like this.

Then with a howl of rage, Godfrey lashed out with his whip, and kept on lashing, so much so that his father jumped down from his horse in alarm and shouted, "No, Godfrey, no."

But his son paid no heed and kept advancing on Tom, who could only retreat. Further and further he was pushed back, until he was up against the water trough, his shirt torn and bloodied.

They were still shouting at one another, but James could not make out the words.

Suddenly, with a final vicious movement, Godfrey shoved Tom hard in the chest. The momentum carried him over the edge of the trough and his head struck the stone surround with a sickening crack.

A gaping wound appeared in the side of his head and blood gushed out of it to run down over his shoulder, to mingle with the water in which he lay.

There was a deathly silence.

Even Godfrey seemed stunned at what he had done.

James was first to move. He thrust open the stable door with such force it rocked on its hinges, and ran across the yard to where his friend lay. He stopped just short of the trough, fear preventing him from going closer.

Slowly, everyone started moving towards the inert body draped grotesquely across the blood-stained stone.

James felt himself go weak and gripped the rough, cold edge. "NO!" He heard the scream from afar. Sobs rasped from his lungs, but he did not know it.

Mr Bates, his face a mask of hate, turned on Godfrey. "You bastard, you've killed him."

Godfrey blanched. "I-I ... No. No, I can't have. He's not dead, he can't be." He looked around wildly for his father, seeking support. But the man was motionless and silent with shock.

"You'd better leave this yard, now." Mr Bates was struggling to control himself. "Now, do you hear me. I don't care who you are, I don't ever want to set eyes on you ever again, or I won't be responsible for my actions."

"That'll do Bates, I'll sort this out," Mr Wytherley-Jones said, regaining his senses and trying desperately to find a way out of the situation. He turned sharply to his son, "Come, Godfrey. With me." And then they both hurried out of the yard, without a backward glance, to leave an anguished circle of men standing around the water-trough.

By now, James had taken one of Tom's hands in his own, surprised at its warmth. His dear friend. Please God, he prayed, let this all be a bad dream. Let me wake up to find Tom still here, still grinning, still fussing the horses.

He heard Mr Bates give out orders to Joe, Fred and Sam. The latter was despatched to fetch the doctor and vicar, while the others would do what they could to help Gretel.

69

He felt his hand being gently removed from Tom's and was dimly aware of being led away. His cold stiff fingers were placed around a mug of steaming tea and a blanket placed around his shivering body. He looked up through tear-misted eyes to see who was taking such good care of him.

To his amazement, it was Mr Bates. The stern faced, hard taskmaster of a man, who had made his life a misery on numerous occasions, was showing that he did have a heart after all.

He spoke quietly. "I'm sorry, lad. I know Tom was your friend. Dreadful thing to happen, but don't expect any punishment for that thug, his sort don't get their come-uppence, not in this life, anyway." He shook his head sadly, "The likes of him, they treat the lower classes with contempt, and get away with it. All we can do is put up with it, if we're to keep our jobs." He grinned ruefully. "That's if I've still got one. Mind, I shall be looking for another position, anyway. I couldn't stay here now."

James just nodded dumbly.

"You'd best get off home, now." Mr Bates said gently, "I think you've had enough for one day. Gretel will be alright, I think, although it may take a while." He blew out between clenched teeth. "Made my blood boil when I saw her. I just wish I'd tried harder to stop Tom, but I never thought it would come to this."

Woodenly, James stood up, placed the blanket back in its place and walked out through the gateway without another word to anyone. He didn't care if he never saw the place again. The pain in his chest increased as he walked home, his mind in turmoil.

To his dismay, the cottage was empty.

In desperation he ran back down the lane and across the fields to find his boyhood perch on the five-bar gate where he sat and gave vent to his feelings.

Only the rolling, green fields heard his cries as he called for answers. Why Tom? Why? His dear friend at work and at leisure. And now too, so soon after Mr Butler….

Time passed unnoticed, but still the knot of grief would not ease. He recalled the past few years and realised that both Tom and Mr Butler had been a large piece of his life. What would he do now?

At last, as the sun dipped low, bringing a chill to the air, he set off homeward. His hair was still matted with whitewash and his shirt had dried hard, but these things went unnoticed.

Never had he felt so alone and helpless.

Chapter Nine

After a sleepless night, James had come to a decision.

"Ma, would yer understand if I decide not to go to work at the stables again?

His mother wrinkled her brow and carried on stirring the broth bubbling in the large pan hung over the fire. "Well, I think yer should give it more thought first."

"I really don't think I can face the place ever again. I need time off to go to Mr Butler's funeral, anyway." He felt a coward, but no other option presented itself.

"Yer'll 'ave to get somethin' else soon."

"Yeh, I know." How could he explain to anyone that the yard would feel haunted, would always carry the nightmarish vision of Tom's lifeless body laying in the horse trough.

His mother had been horrified when told of the incident and of Godfrey Wytherley-Jones. "The likes o' them ain't fit to walk the earth," she had said.

A funeral was the last thing James wanted to go to, and had it been anyone other than Mr Butler he would not have bothered. Even the thought of seeing Mary Ann could barely raise his spirits. But he washed his hair and put on his best clothes just the same.

The afternoon was hot and the sun hung in a brilliant blue sky. James could not help feeling that this was not the most appropriate weather. How could the sun shine so brightly when his heart felt so leaden?

The church was almost half full when he and his mother arrived. They made their way to an empty pew near the back, several people nodding and smiling to them, no doubt surprised to see members of the Newland family in the church as they were not regular attenders.

The peace and beauty of the surroundings had a calming effect on James. He studied the soft colours of the stone and the brightness of the stained-glass windows, and could feel the stirrings of an inner strength begin to creep over him.

He glanced sideways at his mother. She was sitting, hands in lap, eyes closed and looking composed and at ease. He wondered how she did it. Then he remembered that his parents had been married here.

Perhaps she was praying for her husband and son still away in Winchester, or Ellen and her baby.

He marvelled, not for the first time, at her strength. She had been through many rough times over the years and yet, somehow, she carried on. He wished that he was more like her.

She must have sensed him looking, because she opened her eyes and smiled. "You alright, son?" she whispered.

He nodded, and smiled back, feeling even closer to her. Then he wondered suddenly how Tom's mother was coping with his death. Tears threatened, but his attention was brought abruptly back to the present as the vicar's voice broke the silence, asking them all to stand.

He looked across towards the door. The coffin, carried by four men, proceeded into the church. Mrs Butler, Charlotte and Mary Ann walked slowly behind it.

As the vicar led the tiny procession up the aisle, James only had eyes for one person. Mary Ann. He caught his breath and his heart missed a beat at the sight of her. In spite of the sombre occasion, she looked beautiful.

Sorrow and joy mingled inside him, until he felt he could stand it no longer. His legs turned to jelly and it was only with the utmost willpower that he stopped himself from actually fainting clean away.

When at last the service finished and everyone walked slowly out into the sunshine, James took a deep breath and leaned against the porchway wall before following the burial party along the narrow path to Mr Butler's last resting place.

As the vicar intoned the committal Mrs Butler was sobbing, and although her daughter stood beside her, it was Mary Ann who had an arm around the old woman's shoulders and whispered words of comfort.

James could not take his eyes from her face and noticed a tear slide unchecked down her cheek. The urge to go to her was overwhelming, but he daren't. It was not the done thing and everyone would be appalled, especially her mother. Charlotte never missed a chance to let him know what she thought of him.

His mother caught his eye and frowned. "Are yer sure ye're alright, son? Yer look all in." This broke his reserve and the pent up tears welled up in his grey eyes and overflowed. He dashed them away almost angrily. What would Mary Ann think of him? Why, oh why, do I bother? He remonstrated with himself. She'll never look at me, anyway. Even in the plain grey dress and unadorned straw hat she looked wonderful. Why should she notice him?

As the coffin was lowered slowly into the grave, James bade his silent farewell. His mother held on to his arm in support. Unaware of his feelings for Mary Ann she assumed that it was his sorrow at losing Mr Butler and Tom which was upsetting him.

They stood back to allow the funeral party to move away, but to James' surprise Mrs Butler came across to where he stood with his mother and, smiling bravely, put out her hand to grasp his shoulder.

"Thank you for coming, James, and you Mrs Newland, I do appreciate it. We all do," she said, inclining her head to her daughter and granddaughter. "I am going back to Froyle to stay with Charlotte for a while. I might even stay for good, but I'll let you know."

"G'bye, Mrs Butler. We'll miss yer, try not to stay away." James could not imagine being unable to visit Honeysuckle Cottage almost every day from now on.

Then to his joy Mary Ann came to stand beside her grandmother, and to his rapture she spoke to him. "Hello James. I know grandfather would have been glad you were here. You..."

She was prevented from saying more by her mother, who pulled at her arm and glared at James and his mother. "Come away girl, we have to be going. Come along mother."

"See you soon," said Mrs Butler, and her granddaughter turned to wave and gave James a brilliant smile before she too was pushed out of the gateway and into the waiting carriage.

He stood transfixed while his mother muttered something about 'a nasty piece of work that Charlotte,' unaware of her son's mixed emotions.

As they walked home, he was hardly aware of his mother's conversation. More worrying thoughts entered his mind. What if Mrs Butler decided to stay in Froyle? He might never see her or, more importantly, Mary Ann ever again.

His mother noticed his pre-occupation. "I think yer should get to yer bed, son. All these shocks 'ave got to yer."

"No, it's alright ma. I've got to go and visit Tom's parents yet." He let out a long sigh. "I ain't lookin' forward to that mind, but 'as to be done, it's only right."

He didn't see the worried look on his mother's face as she turned her attention to getting the evening meal ready.

His dreams that night were disturbed, bringing unrefreshing, fitful sleep. One minute there were Mary Ann's laughing blue eyes, and the next there were Tom's brown ones. He awoke in a panic after a dream in which he could not remember what Tom looked like. There followed a series of vivid tableaux, one in which the bright church windows cast coloured patterns on a blood-spattered stone floor, and another where the vicar, in flowing black robes, was chasing him towards an open grave. As he pitched forward and was engulfed by the blackness, he awoke shaking.

After that, he tried concentrating on Mary Ann's blue eyes—and at last a more restful sleep overtook him.

Tom's funeral was an ordeal. His mother, sister and the young woman he had been courting, all wailed uncontrollably. The father seemed unable to comfort them, standing on his own and looking lost.

James wept silently into his hands, not caring who saw. It was too painful to keep inside. Fred, Joe, Sam and Mr Bates were all there, and once the committal had taken place Mr Bates went across to have a few words with Tom's parents.

The mother's face turned to fury as he spoke, and she screamed at him as he tried to press something into her hands. The father, by now more in control, took her by the arm and led her away, glancing over his shoulder to give the manager a look of loathing.

Mr Bates came back to stand beside James. "Blood money," he said bitterly. "Wytherley-Jones thinks he can buy off his son's sins with a few sovereigns. Still, they're going to need it—I think Tom was the main breadwinner." He shook his head sadly. "What about you? Are you coming back to the yard?" He looked at James questioningly.

"I'm none too sure yet, to be 'onest. I can't think proper at the moment."

Mr Bates nodded. "Fair enough, I'll leave it up to you. Come back on Monday morning if you can. If not..." He shrugged, then said "I'd just like to say that I would be pleased if you'd stay on. You're good with the horses... Still as I say, it's up to you." He turned and hurried away, leaving James to stand and wonder.

He had never really got on with the man, and yet he had been good to him when Tom was killed. Perhaps there was more to Frank Bates than met the eye.

Perhaps it was worth reconsidering his position—perhaps he should stay on. He had the weekend to think about it, and maybe if his father and Arthur returned home soon he could discuss it with them.

There were a few shocks awaiting them on their return to Selborne and James hoped that they at least could bring some good news. The family could certainly do with it.

Chapter Ten

But it was not to be. Later that same evening John and Arthur Newland arrived home with more bad tidings. John went to his wife and took both her hands.

"I'm sorry dear, we did our best, but it weren't good enough. They wouldn't let us see Ellen afore 'er trial, an' the assize judge were a right nasty so-an'-so. 'E wouldn't let us see 'er after either. 'Cos she 'ad no proper rep-resent-ative," he faltered over the unfamiliar word, "'e wouldn' listen to 'er side o' the story. We tried to plead for 'er, what with the baby an' all, but were no good." His face was ravaged and he struggled to hold his tears in check. "I'm sorry, I've let yer down." He stared down at his feet and James feared that there was worse to come.

His father cleared his throat nervously. "There's no easy way to put this. She's to be transported."

There was a stunned silence.

John Newland put it into plain words for them, "Our Ellen, an' 'er baby are to be sent off on a ship to t'other side of the world." He gulped hard.

Ann Newland slumped onto the fireside chair. "Oh, my poor girl." The words were whispered, disbelief clear on her face.

The tiny kitchen took on an air of unreality. The cosy, lamp-lit scene of three men standing around the slight figure of a woman sitting in front of a blazing fire, belied the truth.

"Didn't they even let yer see the baby, John?"

"'Fraid not, but we did speak to a woman watchin' the female prisoners. She said the little girl's name was Mary. Very small though, an' Ellen's terrible thin. To be expected, I 'spose." He took Ann's hand again. "This woman did say she would tell Ellen we was there, an' she was goin' to give 'er the four pennies I passed over. Just 'ope she did."

The alternative was unthinkable. Ellen would assume no one cared, not even her own family.

James tried to imagine what it must be like, being all alone, accused of something you hadn't done and then being sent to the other side of the world. His mind refused to take any more. He sat

76

down at the table and put his head in his hands, and Arthur came and placed a hand on his shoulder in an uncharacteristic act of comfort.

"When is she to go?" James whispered.

"They'll be takin' 'er to Portsmouth an' puttin' 'er on one o' them prison ships 'til it sails. Pretty soon I should think." Arthur said.

"She ain't goin' to that place where they sent the rioters, is she?"

His father nodded and said, "Australia—Van Diemen's Land."

And Ann Newland had still to tell her husband about Mr Butler, and James gave him the news about Tom.

John Newland shook his head slowly. "What a dreadful time— don't seem possible it's all 'appened at once."

James prayed for his sister and her baby that night, hoping that she knew she was loved and remembered. What an unfair world they lived in. There was no justice for the working classes. Tom and Mr Butler were gone from his life forever, but Ellen was sailing into the unknown all alone with a tiny baby to look after. He screwed up his eyes: 'Lord have mercy on them'.

On Monday morning, much to his mother's relief, James returned to the stables. Joe and Fred slapped him on the back warmly and told him that Gretel would be fine once she had rested a little longer.

Better still, Mr Bates called them into his office with a smile, which was even more unusual. "I thought you'd like to know that the Wytherley-Jones have gone—yes, I thought you'd be pleased. To be honest, so am I. Nice to see you back, Newland." With that, he waved them away. "Now I've work to do."

And James threw himself into it, glad in the knowledge that he would never have to see Godfrey Wytherley-Jones again.

For the first few days he avoided the water trough, but gradually the awful scene faded from his mind until, at last, he was able to touch the stone-work and remember Tom as he had been when still alive. Full of life and full of fun. He would never forget his friend, not as long as he lived.

The stable soon drifted into its new routine. Things had changed … and so had the people. Tom's position was never filled, and Frank Bates became a fairer and much friendlier boss. He made sure that Gretel had the best of care and was adamant that she must never be ridden again.

A month later Ann Newland gave her son what seemed to be more bad news. Mrs Butler was going to stay in Froyle with Charlotte and Mary Ann.

This set James thinking long and hard as to how, and when, he was going to get to Froyle. He would need a horse, that was for sure. Perhaps the new-found heart in Frank Bates could be touched just a little more? It was worth a try.

His father had told him it was about nine miles away, but not difficult to find. "It'll only take about half-an-hour at a canter," he had said with a twinkle in his eye. But this had gone unnoticed by James, whose mind was on other things.

He thought that perhaps he should have a better reason for going than just to see a girl, so he asked his mother if she had any messages for Mrs Butler. "I'd like to go and see her," he said.

He did not see the smile at her lips as she said, "Well, let me see. We could do with some homemade jam, or..." she smiled broadly, "or maybe, you could just go and see how she is."

James looked at his mother doubtfully. "It don't make a very good excuse, do it?"

"Why do you need an excuse? She's our friend, you've known 'er all yer life."

"Well, I was goin' to ask Mr Bates if I could borrow an 'orse. I thought 'e'd want to know why."

"Don't be so feeble son, just ask. He'll say yes or no, then yer can decide what else yer can do."

She made it sound so simple, but she was right, of course. As usual.

So the following morning, he walked into the office and waited for Mr Bates to finish off what he was doing, before putting in his request.

"When were you thinking of going then? I can't let you go in working hours."

Much to James relief, he hadn't refused out of hand. "I were wonderin' if I could go on me Sunday off. I could be exercising one o' the 'orses." He waited with baited breath.

Frank Bates rubbed his chin thoughtfully. "Mm... I think Solomon could perhaps do with some longer runs, he's not getting out much at the moment. You'd have to take great care of him, of course."

James could not believe his ears. It had been so easy. He thanked Mr Bates profusely, leaving the man with a puzzled expression on his face, and rushed off to tell first Solomon and then Gretel the good news.

His day off was still more than a week away and James fretted as time seemed to pass with impossible slowness.

He let his mind wander over his relationship with Mary Ann and her mother, and suddenly remembered that he had not asked his father to tell his side of the story regarding the village riots.

Sitting quietly with him one evening, he put the question.

John Newland studied his son for a few moments and puffed on his old clay pipe before speaking. "What did Mr Butler tell yer?" He asked at last.

James retold the story as best he could. So much had happened in the last few weeks, it seemed a lifetime ago since he had heard it.

His father again sat in silence, obviously deep in thought.

James studied the face in front of him. It was deeply lined now and the white skin showed up against the tan at his temples. Grey hairs were becoming more plentiful among the dark brown too. Poor pa, he thought, is ageing fast.

"Well, 'e seems to 'ave given yer a pretty good account," his father said. "I wasn't really involved that much—just wanted to let folk see I was with 'em. I didn't 'old with the violence." He smiled, "Mind, the old army bugle came in 'andy, I must say. All the noise though—an' to be 'onest, the ale—made me feel right poorly." He tapped his head lightly with a forefinger. "War wound, yer know."

James raised his eyebrows. "I didn't know yer was wounded in the war, pa?"

"I was shot in 'thirteen. Quite bad at the time it was, but soon mended." He leaned back in his chair. "Look, don't worry, son. Most folk in the village was pleased for me—there are only a few 'oo still carry a grudge. It 'appens, some people can never see both sides of anythin'."

"But pa, weren't yer proud to 'ave taken part?"

"I would 'ave been, if it 'ad done any good. But as it was…" He shook his head. With this, James had to be content. His father did not seem to place much importance on his part in the proceedings, but James decided he was proud of him anyway.

At last his Sunday off arrived. He was up early and feeling far too excited to eat, but his mother made sure he'd had two thick slices of bread, spread with bramble jam, before he left.

He was early, and thought it would be nice to ride the horse along the quiet country lanes at a leisurely pace. But on his arrival at the stables, he was surprised to see Mr Bates already in Gretel's stall, giving her a gentle grooming.

"Morning Newland." He called.

"Mornin' Mr Bates. Alright if I saddle up Solomon?"

"Go ahead. It's a nice morning you've got. Visiting Mrs Butler isn't it?"

"I promised 'er I'd go an' see 'er after 'er 'usband died. I do miss 'avin' 'em living near us." Then as he entered Solomon's stall he thought of the real reason for his visit, and brightened considerably.

He chatted quietly to the horse as he worked putting on the tack and saddle, pleased to see that Gretel was getting such good attention too. He'd told Solomon and Gretel all his thoughts and worries during the darkest days, and they'd been his consolation.

So preoccupied was he, that he didn't hear Mr Bates enter. "Would you like a mug of tea before you go? It's quite early yet."

James was too surprised to answer with more than a brief, "Thanks," but once he was sitting in the office, mug in hand, he knew there was something he had to say to Mr Bates. He cleared his throat while he tried to find the right words. "I want yer to know as 'ow I appreciated what yer did for me the day Tom died. I should 'ave said afore, but…" He trailed off lamely.

"Think nothing of it." Mr Bates pulled a tight smile. "It was the least I could do. You looked so shocked, to be honest I feared for your health. It made me realise how lucky I was to have such a good team working for me." James thought he saw the start of a tear in the man's eye at this. "For a man to give his life in the name of humanity, is very humbling. Tom will never be forgotten, I know. He was a very brave, if foolish, young man."

They finished their tea in companionable silence and James felt as though he had found another friend, albeit an unlikely one.

Solomon's impatient stamping brought him to his feet, "Well better be off. I will look after 'im yer know."

"I wouldn't have let you take him if I'd thought anything else," said Frank Bates, smiling.

And so James set off for Froyle sitting astride Solomon. He could hardly believe he was on his way at last. And what a wonderful day to be going to see Mary Ann. Sunshine and white puffs of cloud, and from his position high on the horse's back he could see over the tops of the high hedges and on across the rolling fields beyond.

The clip-clop of the horse's hooves and the soft breeze against his cheeks were a balm to his soul. The troubles and unhappiness of the past few weeks seemed to drift away from him and he could look forward to seeing Mary Ann and Mrs Butler again. He missed them both dreadfully.

Following his father's instructions, after skirting the town of Alton he found a wooden sign-post pointing the way to Froyle. His heart skipped a beat at the sight of the name. He was so close now— he would see her soon.

As he set off down the tree-lined lane, he had a strange feeling of being cut off from the rest of the world, of unreality.

How far now? he wondered. Then, at last, bright sunshine lit up a row of cottages there before him, edging a small green. Further along the lane he could see a church, and in front stood a few lone figures.

He was just about to go to them and ask if anyone knew Mrs Butler, when he saw two women emerge from the cottage nearest to him. And the world stood still for an instant as he realised that they were the very people that he had come to see.

He paused, savouring the sight of Mary Ann, and drinking in her beauty. It might have been better if they had been aware of his intention to visit, he knew, but he'd been afraid Charlotte Knight would have tried to stop it.

Sliding down from the saddle he walked towards them, wondering how close he could get before they caught sight of him. They both saw him in the same instant and turned to him, wreathed in smiles. He broke into a run and covered the short distance in seconds.

"Oh, James, how lovely. What a surprise!" Mrs Butler clapped her hands with joy.

Mary Ann seemed a little shy, but smiled warmly. "Hello, James," she whispered.

He wanted to take her hands in his, wanted to tell her he loved her, but he knew that it would never do; even Mrs Butler would frown on such uncouth behaviour.

She was asking him now, "What are you doing here? Have you ridden all this way just to see us?"

James found his tongue at last and laughed. "Of course I came to see you—both of you. The 'orse needed exercisin' so 'ere I am. How are you? Yer lookin' well Mrs Butler—an' yer lookin' right pretty, Mary Ann," he said, making her blush.

"We're fine, lad, fine. I've settled in alright here, but I do miss my friends in Selborne. Mary Ann is a good companion to me. We do

81

have some lovely times, don't we?" Her granddaughter was still blushing. "We're just off to church, lad, otherwise I'd ask you in for a cup o' tea or something, seeing as you've come all that way." She seemed a little uncomfortable at the thought of being inhospitable.

"That's alright, I understand." James reassured her.

Mary Ann was about to speak, when her mother came hurrying out of the gateway—she was not at all happy to see him.

Completely ignoring James, she took hold of her daughter's arm and pulled her away, saying angrily, "What do you think you are doing? Talking to riff-raff in the streets—and you should know better, mother. Hurry up, we'll be late for church," and she turned and marched off along the pathway, dragging Mary Ann with her.

Mrs Butler stood, open-mouthed, at her daughter's rudeness. "Oh, how could she. I am sorry lad. That's unforgivable."

"Never mind—you'd better be off, or you'll 'ave 'er shoutin' at yer some more. I'll come again. Look after yerself—an' Mary Ann."

She shot him a knowing look. "G'bye lad. Give my regards to yer ma and pa." Then with a little wave she hurried after her daughter's retreating figure. And much to James' delight, Mary Ann managed to turn and give him one of her lovely smiles before being dragged out of sight.

He stood watching until they were inside the church, and then for a while longer, trying to make sense of Charlotte's behaviour. A horrible woman, he thought. Why did she hate him so?

He remounted Solomon and set off, back the way he had come. Was he less joyful? He had seen his love and he cherished the memory of her smile. He kept in mind how becoming she had looked in the fine blue cotton dress which matched the colour of her eyes, and the straw bonnet tied with a matching ribbon beneath her dainty chin.

He felt refreshed and happier than he had been in a long time. Even Charlotte's churlishness could not dampen his spirits, but he was determined to find out just what it was that upset the woman.

After stabling Solomon and giving both him and Gretel the treat of an apple, he set off home to seek out his mother. She would be the one to advise him. She had been through so much over the years, and even more in the past few weeks, but somehow she seemed able to take whatever knocks life threw at her and still come out smiling. With her wisdom she would help him, he knew.

Back at the cottage, he surprised his parents and two sisters as they were eating lunch.

"You're back early son. There's some stew in the pot though, help yerself." His mother looked at him, the unasked questions clear in her eyes.

James filled a mug with water from the ewer and gulped it down before helping himself to food and seating himself at the table.

"I'm back early 'cause Mrs Butler's daughter were really rude and dragged 'er, Mrs Butler that is, an' Mary Ann off to church without so much as a 'good mornin'. Riff-raff she called me. Bloomin' cheek."

His sisters cast knowing looks at each other. He knew he shouldn't have said anything in front of them, for it would be all round the village now. But his mother had seen it too.

"Right, you two, get that sewin' finished or yer'll 'ave nothin' t' wear. An' don't go blabbin' our business outside this 'ouse. Do yer 'ear me."

Sheepishly the two girls nodded and went outside to finish their needlework in the sunshine.

Once alone with his parents, James was more forthcoming. "I really can't understand what she's got against me. I know I ain't good enough for the likes o' Mary Ann, but 'er ma don't 'ave to be so nasty. Poor Mrs Butler were right embarrassed." He lapsed into silence while his father repeated more or less what Mr Butler had told him that evening on the porch.

"Yeh, but she's 'ad Mary Ann since then, ain't she?" James looked from one to the other.

"He's right John. There's more to this than meets the eye." Ann Newland said, as she cleared the dishes from the table. "I think Mrs Knight is getting above her station. I wonder why."

Harriet came into the kitchen, sewing basket in hand, "We've finished ma—can we go out for a walk?"

"Alright, but don't go too far, mind—an' no 'angin' round the village boys." She spoke firmly, but once the girls were out of earshot she laughed, "Might as well tell the sun not to shine."

John Newland nodded, "As long as they don't bring no trouble 'ome—we've 'ad enough o' that to last a lifetime."

His wife sighed. She looked across to where James was sitting deep in thought. "Try not to worry son. Look, I know Mary Ann means a lot to yer, but she very young yet. Why, she can't be any more than fourteen—just give it time. Things can change an' yer can still go to see Mrs Butler now and again, to keep in touch."

John Newland looked from his wife to his son. "There you are lad, listen to yer ma. She always talks sense, yer know that. It's why I married 'er..." He ducked as a wooden spoon flew past his ear.

The mood had lightened and James felt more at ease again. Everything would be alright in the end, he was sure. Except for... He spoke almost without thinking, "I wonder 'ow Ellen is," and instantly regretted it.

The shadows, so skilfully dispelled by his parents, were back.

"No, James, don't even think about it." His mother seemed to know what he was going to say. "She isn't allowed any visitors, we've checked. Now leave it." She was nearly in tears.

He was full of remorse, "I'm sorry ma, I didn't think." That was the trouble, he scolded himself, he didn't think before he spoke. "I'll make meself useful in the garden," he said, and escaped through the door.

Chapter Eleven

Mary Ann's laughter filled the air, competing with the birdsong. She was leaning against an open gate, where the field met the lane. Her grandmother stood next to her holding an empty basket. It was nearly time to go.

James felt his stomach contract. Three years later, and now today was the day. They had talked it over, Mrs Butler, Mary Ann and himself. Today he was going to ask Charlotte Knight for her daughter's hand in marriage. She would not like it, and most likely would refuse point blank. But he was willing to take the chance.

They had been very patient, waiting as long as they had. Almost every Sunday, once a month—except in very inclement weather—James had ridden over to Froyle to see Mary Ann. Mrs Butler had been a willing and adept conspirator, arranging to bring out a picnic on fine days, like today, and when it was wet, they sat in the church porch, a large closed one. He never stayed much more than an hour, but their meetings were pure delight, for both of them.

If Charlotte was aware of his visits, she showed no signs—and as Mrs Butler had said, she firmly believed that she did not, otherwise she would not have let Mary Ann out.

This made James' task even more daunting. He had only seen Charlotte once since their encounter on that first day, and that event had been equally unpleasant. He had been riding along the lane leading to the village when she passed by in a small carriage and, seeing who it was, shook her fist out of the window. This had frightened Solomon, but luckily he was a steady horse and James had not been in any danger—however, she had meant him no good.

And now here he was, about to ask her if he could marry her daughter. He must be mad. Everyone said so. His parents, Frank Bates and even Mrs Butler, although she had said that she was glad and would like nothing better than to see them married.

Mary Ann held out her hand and he took it in his own, giving her a smile of encouragement. His heart missed a beat, as it usually did when he saw in her eyes the love for him returned.

"Are you ready, James? I'm sure when mother sees how much we love each other, she'll understand."

He pressed her hand to his chest, "If it comes to the worst, you'll wait for me, won't you?" he asked.

"Oh, James, there'll never be anyone else. I'll wait, I promise."

Mrs Butler wiped a tear from her eyes. "Come on you two and just remember, I'm on your side."

They set off walking three abreast down the lane. No one spoke, although Mary Ann gave James' arm a squeeze from time to time. He was surprised at the firmness of her touch, and it gave him strength. The best was worth fighting for.

Then the cottage came into sight and his heart sank to his boots, his legs turned to jelly and he wondered if he'd make it up the short path.

Mrs Butler lifted the latch and pushed open the door. "Hello, Charlotte, we've got a visitor," she called.

James followed her into the dim interior, but before he could speak he heard Charlotte's sharp voice say, "What's he doing here?"

It did not bode well and he nearly took flight there and then, but managed a polite, "Good afternoon, Mrs Knight." He cleared his throat, with the intention of continuing, but before he could, Charlotte broke in.

"What do you think you're doing?" She had risen from her chair looking swiftly from her daughter to her mother, her face dark and wary.

"Mother, this is James. We want to ask you something." Mary Ann tried to keep her voice even.

"Mrs Knight, I want to ask you for your daughter's hand. I want her to be my wife." The effort of moderating his broad country vowels stretched his already taut nerves.

Charlotte's face was crimson. "How dare you—you upstart! If you think I'd ever agree to a marriage between you two, you must be mad." She gave a sharp laugh, without any trace of humour. "I think you'd better go ... and don't dare come back." She shot a look at her mother, "Did you know about this?"

"Of course," Mrs Butler said. "You could at least hear the lad out, Charlotte. He's worked hard and has a secure job ... and they're so much in love."

"Love," spat out Charlotte. "What do they know about love?" She spun on James again. "If you think I would let a daughter of mine marry riff-raff like you, you must be more stupid than you look." She glared at her daughter, "Get to your room, I'll deal with you later."

"But mother, please listen to James. I've loved him for so long. He's good and kind, look how much he helped grandfather. He's not common or rough, he's…" Mary Ann burst into tears and James moved to comfort her, but Charlotte stepped in between them and dragged her daughter away.

Mrs Butler tried again to plead their case. "Mary Ann is right, you know, and the lad has behaved himself well. They have never met without me present to chaperone. And anyway, I've always felt that James was almost family. Your grandfather thought the world of him. Mary Ann could do a lot worse."

"Worse! I hope that she will do a whole lot better. She is not going to marry some country bumpkin and saddle herself with hordes of screaming brats." She moved a few inches towards James. "That is my final word on the subject, so now get out." The threat in her voice was unmistakable.

James looked at Mary Ann, wanting to take her hand and run away with her, but he knew the sensible thing to do was to leave quietly, before the situation got out of hand. He would not put himself in a good light by being childish or hasty.

"Right, I'll go … for now, but I'll be back. I won't give up. I'll never love anyone else and even if I have to wait till she's twenty-one, then wait I will." He threw a loving look at Mary Ann. "We will be together some day…" Tears threatened, but he took a deep breath and spoke to Mrs Butler. "Thanks for all yer 'elp. I hope I'll see yer soon."

He stepped backward the two paces it took to regain the doorstep and turned and walked away down the path, Mary Ann's cries ringing in his ears.

The door was slammed shut behind him.

How he got himself to where Solomon was tethered and rode home he never knew. The pain in his chest was all-consuming—worse even than when Tom had died, and that had been bad enough.

Why was Charlotte Knight so against him? Why? He must find out the reason—there had to be an answer. He fretted about Mary Ann, about leaving her there with her hard-faced mother. He hoped that she was not being punished. But no, surely Mrs Butler would intervene.

But still he worried, and by the time he reached home his head throbbed and he felt physically sick.

As he entered the cottage, his mother jumped to her feet. "Whatever's wrong? Yer look terrible. Here sit down." She pushed gently at his shoulder.

His father also looked concerned. They knew where he had been, and for what reason. "Gave yer a bad time, did she?" he asked.

James nodded. "I don't know what 'er problem is, 'onest I don't. I knew that she didn't like me, but she were so nasty."

He related in detail what had taken place.

"Oh, that poor girl ... and Mrs Butler. Life can't be easy for them living with that woman. I'd like to give 'er a piece o' my mind." Ann Newland said fiercely.

"Don't yer go upsettin' yerself," John said to his wife. "That ain't goin' to 'elp anybody."

They sat in silence for a while, each occupied with their own thoughts.

Then, John Newland broke his reverie. "I know 'oo might be able to 'elp."

His wife looked up in surprise. "Who do yer mean?"

"Well, yer know old Job, as works in the dairy? 'E knows more 'bout folk in this village than they knows 'emselves." He chuckled, "The stories 'e tells... I'll go an' see 'im and see if 'e can throw any light on the subject."

James frowned. "No pa, it don't seem right, to go askin' questions 'bout people. I'll sort somethin' yer'll see."

He did not see the wink his father gave his mother.

Mary Ann lay sobbing on her bed, with Mrs Butler gently stroking the damp hair from her brow.

"Why is mother so against James, gran? After all, I know we live better than his family, but that's only because my father pays for it. We're still ordinary people underneath, aren't we?"

Mrs Butler wrinkled her brow. "I wish I knew, dear, I really do. He's such a lovely young man, you'd think she'd be pleased for you. Money and clothes aren't everything, after all."

"What do you think she'll do now?" The girl asked, "She won't send me away, will she?"

"I shouldn't think so—where could she send you? Not to your father, that's for sure."

"No, he'd never want the bother of me, and I'd hate living in London anyway." She thought for a while. "I know, I'll run away, that's what I'll do. I'm sure James' family would let me live with them. I'd like to live in Selborne." A smile lit her face, "You could come with me, gran."

Mrs Butler patted her hand, "My dear girl if you do that, your mother will have you dragged back here in no time. With or without me. You're only seventeen. I'm sorry dear," she kissed Mary Ann's soft, pink cheek, "but you'll just have to be patient." And with another kiss and a smile, she left the young girl to her day-dreams.

It was several days later before John Newland could see old Job, because the man had been ill. Then one evening he went to visit him, taking half a sackfull of potatoes and carrots from his garden as a present.

"'Allo, John, what a surprise—it's nice to see yer." He eyed the sack. "What yer got there then?"

"I thought as 'ow yer could do with a some veg, Job. I know things get a bit tight when you're not at work."

The old man grinned, showing blackened, rotting teeth with a considerable number of gaps. "Cor, that's kind o' yer." He rubbed his hands together. "We'll look forward to some o' your tatties. Come in a minute, if yer got time."

"Thanks, I will." John studied him and realised why he had been off work so long—he looked terrible. "'Ow old are yer now Job?" he asked.

"Well, don't rightly know fer sure. Somewhere about eighty, I think." He cackled and motioned John to a chair.

"When do yer think yer'll be back at work then?"

The old man scratched his head, "Dunno—I still don't feel right. Gets a lot o' pains 'ere," he rubbed his chest, "an' I've got the most awful cough. Keeps the missus awake—she don't arf moan." His throaty laugh, gave way to a hacking cough, as though to prove his point.

"Sounds rough, Job. You'd best be stayin' indoors for a while longer."

"Ah, 'spose so—it ain't easy though."

"The other men an' me, we'll bring yer what we can—yer won't starve." John hesitated, the old man was not well. Then he continued, "I 'ope yer feel up to it, but..."

"Yeh?" Job prompted

"Well, we've somethin' of a problem, an' I wondered if yer can shed any light on it." He told Job briefly about Charlotte Knight's attitude to his family. "So yer see, it's a mystery," he concluded.

"Ah well, I might be able to 'elp yer there," Job nodded wisely.

Meanwhile, James was fretting. His next Sunday off could not come soon enough. Although he was head groom now, he still had only one Sunday off a month. Frank Bates was sympathetic, but there was nothing he could do. Staff were scarce, and Fred and Joe had left to go and serve Queen and country with the Royal Hampshire Regiment.

"The best there is," John Newland said proudly when James told him. It was the one in which he had served.

Frank Bates and James had become good friends over the years, starting from the day Tom died—so much so that James was godfather to Frank's eldest daughter.

The stables were a very different place to work now. The family who had replaced the Wytherley-Jones were of a much better class and consisted of Mr and Mrs Wright and their three young children. Mr Wright was liked and respected almost as much as Mr Turner had been, and his standards were just as high, but he expected everything done with the minimum of manpower.

The children loved the horses and were often to be found hanging around the stables. The youngest, a little girl of four, was even allowed to have short rides around the paddock on Gretel with James holding the leading rein. He enjoyed these times and had delighted in telling Mary Ann about the child's antics, and they had sometimes daydreamed about having a daughter—and a pony—of their own one day.

Now that dream would have to be shelved for a while.

He worried that he could not even get a message to her, and cursed himself—not for the first time—for never having learnt to write when at school, but no one had placed much importance on it. Labourers and their families did not need to know such things—that was the general consensus.

The days passed slowly no matter how hard he worked. The evenings were the worst because he had no Mr and Mrs Butler to go and help, and he took to going on long walks around the village. On these he saw many birds, animals and plants remembered from his boyhood, and started keeping mental notes so that he could tell Mary Ann about them when next they met.

Just over two weeks after his unsuccessful visit to Froyle, he arrived home to see his parents deep in conversation.

They looked up as he entered, and his father said solemnly, "I've got a bit o' news son, so sit yer down."

James sat, his heart beating a tattoo inside his ribs. What now?

"Yer'll 'ave to bear with me, 'cos it's not easy to explain, An' don't go jumpin' off yer 'igh 'orse till I've finished." John cleared his throat and rubbed his chin with a fore-finger thoughtfully. "Thing is, we think we know why Mary Ann's ma is against yer." He held up a hand, as James made to interrupt. "'Ear me out. The trouble is it's my fault. Not deliberately of course." He added hastily. "It's the business of the riot rearin' its ugly 'ead again. God, if only yer knew what might 'appen years later, yer'd never do half o' the things yer do when yer young." A loud sigh came from his lips, and James waited with as much patience as he could muster.

"Well, accordin' to old Job, as works up the dairy, Charlotte Butler—as she were then—was set to marry a chap called Thomas 'Ardin', but 'e got involved in the riots. A bit of a fighter as I remember, an' 'e liked 'is ale. Trouble was 'e was one o' them as got transported." He paused, and James butted in.

"Yeh, but that weren't yer fault."

"I told yer, feelin's was runnin' 'igh at the time. My six months in Winchester weren't no bed o' roses, but it were better than bein' sent off away from yer ma an' the little'ns." He grinned. "An' you wouldn't even be 'ere. The families o' those shipped away found things really 'ard—they'd lost their wage-earner, don't forget." He frowned and shook his head, "Can't imagine what caused that woman to be'ave the way she did, but she swore she'd never forgive the ring-leaders o' the mob. Now as yer know I weren't one o' 'em, but made no difference to 'er—'ates us all, she do."

"But she's 'ad Mary Ann since then." James couldn't help thinking that she had not missed this Thomas for long.

"As I was sayin', it don't 'elp that I'm the only one left 'ere for 'er to blame and see the trouble she's causin'. Now, Mary Ann." John took a very deep breath. "That's another story, an' not one she'd be too keen to 'ave made public, I know."

James fixed his attention firmly on his father's face. "Go on pa."

"Alright, alright, give me time." He raised his eyebrows and shot his son a wicked grin. "You might find this interestin'. It could even give yer some leverage." He paused for effect. "Accordin' to Job, she took 'erself off to work for a Mr Knight 'oo lived out on the Alton Road, an' it were 'is son what got Charlotte in the family way. The older Mr Knight were furious an' ordered 'is son to marry the girl. It were all done quiet like—even Mr and Mrs Butler didn't know the truth." He stopped to light his clay pipe, while James sat mesmerised, absorbing this latest information.

"Such a shame," John went on, "their only daughter, an' she does that to 'em. The cottage at Froyle was bought by the father so 'is son could settle, but the young man had no intention of livin' with Charlotte. 'E'd 'ad 'is way with 'er and then didn't want to know— and although he pays fer their keep, 'e's never 'ad any more to do with 'em. Lives up in London, apparently, and because Charlotte's been stood up by 'im, she still feels aggrieved 'bout the lover 'oo she could 'ave 'ad—if the riot 'adn't 'appened, and if I 'adn't blown me trumpet, as she sees it."

James felt his heart swell with love and longing. Poor Mary Ann—what an awful life she must have had: a bitter mother and an absent father.

It explained a lot though, how they lived in better circumstances and were always well dressed. Because of that, Charlotte obviously thought that she was better than everyone else. She seems to have been unaware that some knew her secret.

But he had a weapon. Perhaps now he could get the better of Charlotte Knight; and he could not wait to see her face when he told her that he knew the truth.

Chapter Twelve

James waited impatiently for his next day off. It arrived with lashing rain which turned the road to a quagmire as he made his way to the stables. It was going to be a wet ride, but even that did not dampen his spirits.

Solomon seemed to sense James' inner tension and became quite jittery on the ride to Froyle. The lanes were a quagmire and he had to slow the pace so that the horse could keep a foothold.

He was relieved when the village came into view, but wondered what he could do about the thick mud which caked his legs, not wanting to arrive looking in such a mess. Then he remembered the small stream that ran beside the lane, and sliding down from the saddle, he removed his dripping coat and plunged his hands into the icy cold water. With handfuls of wet grass he endeavoured to remove as much of the mud as possible. The result was not altogether successful, but he sighed resignedly and pushed back his wet hair—he would have to do as he was.

Solomon snickered softly as James took the reins and led him towards the village. There he tethered him to a rail set under a sheltering oak tree. Froyle was very quiet—not many ventured out in such weather it seemed, but he had expected to see some folk on their way to church. An air of gloom seemed to hang over the place, but he dismissed it and marched up to the front door of Charlotte Knight's cottage.

He had rehearsed many times what he was going to say. He would give her a chance to change her mind first, but if she didn't...

He banged on the front door purposefully.

Silence.

He banged again, even louder.

Still silence.

How odd. Then a pang of fear went through him. They could not have gone away, surely Mrs Butler would have sent a message.

He hammered with both hands on the wood, tears of frustration in his eyes.

After several moments, when he knew for certain that no one could be inside, he stood back and looked at the cottage, as though for inspiration.

What could he do?

Then he remembered the old man who lived next door. They had got to know one another over the years because James always admired his garden, and so he went down one pathway and up another.

The old man answered his knock with a toothless smile, "'Ello there. What can I do fer you?"

"I've come to see Mary Ann, but there don't seem to be anyone about. It's still too early for church…" James trailed off, feeling a bit silly now. Why did he always panic?

"Ah, I think they've gone away fer a while. Went off last week, after the funeral."

James heart did a somersault and his insides tightened.

"F-funeral, whose funeral?" He could not breath.

The man looked taken aback. "Oh, sorry, didn't yer know? The old lady it were—real sudden like." He stood looking apologetic. "Sorry," he said again.

James felt his blood freeze. Mrs Butler, his dear, dear friend, dead.

His voice sounded unreal in his ears, "Who could I ask? who might know where they've gone?"

"Best to see the vicar, son. 'E might know. Vicarage is next to the church, but would yer like to come in 'ere first—you've 'ad a nasty shock by the look on yer." He stood back to let James pass. "You're very welcome."

"Thanks, yer very kind, but I'm soakin' wet. I'll get off to see the vicar." He did not know what else to say, but turned as he went and said, "Thanks."

He trudged back down the path in torment. His heart felt like a rock and he found it hard to believe that just a short while ago, he had been filled with such optimism and joy.

Unanswered questions jostled for space in his brain. Where were Mary Ann and her mother now? Why had no one in Selborne been notified of Mrs Butler's death?

He could not imagine life without the lovely old lady, whom he loved almost as much as he did her granddaughter. She had been the one person who had helped himself and Mary Ann through all their years of secret courtship. She had been friend and comforter, steadfast and loyal. His tears mingled with the rain as he made his way to the vicarage.

His knock at the door was answered immediately and a friendly housekeeper showed him straight into a cosy parlour, waving away his apologies for leaving muddy footprints on the tiled floor.

The vicar rose from his seat and extended a hand. "Come in, young man, come nearer to the fire. Hannah," he addressed the woman, "bring some hot tea and a blanket, please."

"Of course, sir." She smiled at James and left.

He was so overcome at the show of kindness, that it was difficult to control his tears. Somehow though, he did not think that this vicar—so very different from the one who had resided at Selborne three years ago—would have minded if he had cried his eyes out.

While they waited for Hannah to bring the tea, he was bidden to remove his jacket, which was placed across the back of a chair where it steamed from the warmth.

"Now, what can I do for you? I know you by sight, but not by name I'm afraid." The pleasant-faced man sat back in his chair and smiled encouragingly.

"Me name is James Newland and I live in Selborne." He hesitated, not knowing how much to tell the man.

"Don't worry, take your time. I can see that you're upset, is it something to do with Mrs Butler?"

James shot him a surprised look. "Why yeh. To be 'onest I'm both sad and angry. I've just been told about Mrs Butler dyin', an' I'm angry that Mrs Knight didn't let anyone know." He rubbed his cold hands across face. "An' now ... she seems to 'ave taken Mary Ann away." Tears filled his eyes, but went unheeded.

The vicar's jaw tightened. "Just as I thought. I did wonder that there were so few people at the funeral of such a pleasant old lady, but when I questioned Mrs Knight about it, she said that none of her mother's friends from Selborne could get here. I wish now that I had sent a message myself." His face darkened. "As to where she has taken her daughter I can't really help you. Refused point blank to tell anyone. Because of you I assume?"

James nodded, "Yeh, because of me."

Just then the tea arrived, accompanied by hot toast, and a warm blanket was tucked snugly around his shoulders.

"Do you want to tell me the whole story?" the vicar invited.

James was worried about Solomon and said that he could not leave him too long, but his mind was put at rest when Hannah was instructed to send her husband out and fetch the horse back to the stable.

Once he had started his story, James could not stop. He had not meant to tell the man everything, but out it all came.

"I am sorry, I had no idea Mrs Knight treated her daughter so unfairly. A delightful young woman—I can see why you love her. The only option I can think of at the moment is for you to wait and see if they return. The cottage has all their belongings still inside— they only took a few clothes." Then with sympathy, "If I hear word of anything, or their whereabouts, I'll let you know. I can send a message to the vicar of Selborne and he can pass it on." He sighed, "Let's hope that it will not be too long, eh!"

"Thank you so much, sir. For everythin' I mean. I feel much better now, so I'd better be gettin' 'ome. I've to tell me ma and pa 'bout Mrs Butler…" He shook his head.

Hannah saw him out and he thanked her too for her kindness. If only everyone were good and kind like those two, the world would be a happier place.

On the ride back home, a battle between sorrow and anger raged within him. Charlotte Knight might think that she had won the day for now, but he would not give up. If it took him the rest of his life, he would find them and bring Mary Ann back to be his wife. How he would do it, he had no idea. He had no knowledge of the outside world and it was a large and daunting place, but he was certain that Mary Ann, wherever she was, was thinking of him just as much as he was of her.

They would be together, some day, some how. They had to be.

Chapter Thirteen

"Well, if it's what you really want, I 'spose there ain't nothin' else to say."

Two years had passed since the day that they had learned of Mrs Butler's death and now John Newland stood in his kitchen and looked in resignation at the two sons in front of him.

His wife sat quietly in her chair, but although she said nothing, James knew that she was upset.

Why did Arthur and William want to go off to war, anyway? Who in their right mind would want to fight a battle in which neither side seemed at all sure what it was they were fighting for?

And so far away—that's why his mother was upset. She had not been much further than Winchester in her life, and it must have felt to her that they would go never to return, just like Ellen.

James was not too sure where the Crimea was, but did not want to prove his ignorance by asking.

Arthur was trying to reassure his parents. "We're sorry. We know yer'll worry, but it's somethin' we want to do. There ain't much goin' for us 'ere." He shrugged and grinned. "All the best girls 'ave been snapped up." Then said on a more serious note, "Works scarce, yer know that."

"You was in the army yerself, pa, so you should know 'ow we feel," said William reasonably.

"I was, an' I was injured too. That weren't a lot o' fun, I can tell yer. Yer don't want to believe everythin' they tells yer down at the signin'-on office, neither." He glanced at his wife. "What do yer think, ma?"

"I think these two are big enough to look after themselves, an' if it's what they really want..." she shrugged, a tight smile lifting the corners of her lips.

William and Arthur looked at each other sheepishly for a moment. None of them liked upsetting their mother.

James let the continuing conversation flow over him, and allowed his thoughts to drift off, as they so often did, to Mary Ann.

He had tried to be patient, but it did not come easily. He had wanted to leave home, take to the roads and wander the countryside looking for her. His mother had pointed out—sensibly, he had to

97

admit—that if he did that and Mary Ann made her way back to Selborne, he would not be here when she arrived.

Besides, they could be anywhere, she had said. England was a big place. He might go one way and she another, and then where would they be? Not together that was for sure.

He knew that she was right. His father too, when he had said that it was best for him to stay put and save his wages for the day she either sent word or turned up.

Time passed so slowly, even though he threw himself into his work and had to help his parents more now that they were not so young. He delighted in the time he spent at Frank Bates' home with his children. He had two little girls now and another baby on the way. James often took them out on walks and helped them learn about the flowers and birds along the pathways as they went.

His heart ached for children of his own, his and Mary Ann's.

The vicar at Froyle had passed messages on several occasions to tell him that Charlotte Knight had been back to the cottage, but never for more than a few days and never over a weekend when she suspected that James might be around.

Now he sat gazing sadly out of the window, while his brothers talked excitedly of going to war.

A few weeks later the Newland family gathered in the tiny kitchen to see the two newly attired soldiers say their farewells.

"My, my—that's the smartest I've ever seen you two look, that's for sure." John laughed. "You'll frighten them Ruskies away with one sight o' you." The pride in his voice was unmistakable.

"I almost wish I was goin' with yer," James said, and everyone laughed when he looked affronted. "What's wrong in that?"

William patted him on the back and between hearty guffaws of laughter said, "Yer'd be no good. Yer'd be stoppin' every few yards to study the flowers, or listen to the birds. Yer'd get yerself shot afore a day were out."

James pulled a face, but smiled because he knew that it was true. He wouldn't be able to shoot someone, or run a bayonet through a living body. No, war was not for the likes of him.

Once the little kitchen had almost emptied, and the young men were on their way, Ann Newland gazed into the fire with tear-filled eyes. "Dear God, please keep my sons safe." She whispered.

More weeks passed, and the cottage was once again filled to over-flowing. The noise was deafening and James wondered how his sisters ever followed a conversation, as they all seemed to talk at once.

The centre of attention today was Eliza's new-born baby. He marvelled at his mother's capacity to love so many grandchildren, no matter how many came along, but James was pleased—it took his mother's mind off thoughts of her children so far away. News from the Crimea was scant, and not very good when it came.

"No news is good news." His father had said.

James, having made a fuss of the new arrival, decided it best to leave the womenfolk to their chatter and was nearly out of the door when he heard something which made his heart miss a beat.

He spun round to face Eliza. "What did you say?"

His sister looked up, not realising what an impact her words had had on him. "I saw Mrs Knight an' 'er daughter in Alton." She told him.

"When? Tell me when?"

"Day afore yesterday, in the mornin' 'twer. I'd gone in on the wagon with John's pa to fetch…"

James cut in. "Why didn't yer tell me, yer know I've been lookin' for 'er," he shouted.

Eliza was taken aback, but shrugged, "Sorry, I didn't think."

James was furious with his sister, and from what he heard his mother saying to the girl as he ran out of the door, so was she.

He raced to the stables, nearly tripping in his haste. Solomon had never been saddled so quickly, and was lucky not to have been ridden bareback, because the thought had crossed James' mind. The young stable lad, still working in the yard, stared at the retreating backs of horse and man open-mouthed.

The journey to Froyle seemed to take an age. If he hadn't known it was impossible, James would have sworn that someone had tacked a dozen extra miles on the road.

The thudding hoofbeats echoed his own heartbeat, and he prayed, harder than he had ever prayed before.

Please let her be there, please.

As he reined in Solomon outside the cottage, his spirits sank. The place was empty. But he walked up the path and peered in through the windows anyway.

The once cosy interior looked bleak and cold, just as James himself felt. He wanted to cry out loud, to smash the place up, anything to let the pain out.

For a while he stood dejectedly in the front garden, not knowing what to do, nor where to go. How would he find her now?

Then the old man who lived next door came out. "Ah, I thought it were you. I can see by yer face yer realise they've gone. Day afore yesterday it were. Real sudden like, just turned up out o' the blue, an' was packed up an' gone in the wink of an eye." The man smiled and James wondered how he could be so cruel. But turning back inside his home, the man said, "'Old on a minute, I've somethin' for yer."

He re-emerged clutching a piece of paper in his grubby hand. "She left this for yer, the young miss." He said, holding it out to James.

A note. Mary Ann had left him a note.

"She scribbled this while 'er ma wasn't lookin'. Upset she were, the young'n. Didn't want to go, but 'er ma, she were real cross, an' dragged 'er to the carriage. Cryin' an' a'carryin' on she were, poor little mite." He shook his head sadly at the memory.

James dashed a tear of his own away. "Thanks fer keeping this fer me, an' fer keepin' an eye out fer me."

"You're welcome, son. We guessed you'd come, when vicar sent word."

"But I didn't get any message," James said. "My sister saw 'em in Alton, that's why I rode over."

"Oh, what a shame. You'd better let 'im know. Mind you, to be 'onest, I doubt if you'd 'ave got 'ere in time. As I said, they was 'ere an' gone so quick."

James thanked the man once more and walked up the lane towards the vicarage, leaving Solomon to chew on the grass verge.

The vicar was friendly and helpful as usual, but annoyed that his message had not been delivered.

"I told the carter to be quick, as it was urgent. I'm sorry lad, but as far as I can tell Mrs Knight has sold the cottage and gone for good this time." He patted James on the shoulder. "Perhaps I'm being over-optimistic, but I feel sure that Mary Ann will find a way to get to you, somewhen. She is still very young yet and her mother rules her with a rod of iron, doesn't let the poor girl out of her sight."

"Please sir, could yer read this fer me. She left a note, an' I can't read…"

"Certainly." He took the small scrap of cream paper and scanned it, before reading aloud what it said:

"Dearest James. I still love you, wait for me. I will be twenty-one in two years time and then mother cannot stop me from being with you. Yours Mary Ann."

He looked at James, his eyes full of pleasure. "It's brief, but at least you know that she still cares. Bless you son for coming to me. I'm pleased to have been of help. Let me know how you get on."

With a weak smile James thanked him and ambled back to his horse. He whispered softly into a large, velvety ear, "She's left me a note, boy. Mary Ann's left me a note. She still loves me."

With aching heart he mounted the horse and set off back to Selborne, and once Solomon was rubbed down and stabled he hurried home to tell his parents what Mary Ann had written.

But two years seemed like a lifetime.

Chapter Fourteen

"Still no word, then?" Frank Bates asked one morning as they cut open some bales of sweet-smelling hay.

"Nah, not yet. Still, 'er birthday ain't until October." James was dejected. The past two years had dragged unbearably, in spite of him working longer and longer hours.

Frank had despaired. "The stalls don't need paintin' again, and the tack-room's like a new pin now, for goodness sake. Will you get yourself off home, man. Go and help someone else, can't you?"

So he had, and some of the older residents of the village had been glad of his help with their gardens, and so pleased with the results, that James was now considered one of the best jobbing gardeners in the area.

Once the horses had been turned out into the paddock, he and Frank went back into the office for a brew of tea.

"Have your parents heard from your brothers at all, lately?"

"Nope. They ain't no letter writers at the best of times, but we've not 'eard anythin' fer months now. Just 'ope they're alright, that's all." James was worried about his mother. "Ma seems so distant sometimes, an' I know pa frets, although 'e don't say much."

"Well, don't raise their hopes, but according to Mr Wright the fighting's stopped."

James stared at his friend. "Really! 'Ow does 'e know that then?"

"He gets newspapers from London, nearly every day, and the one he got yesterday said that the matter was settled in the Crimea."

"Oh, I do 'ope so. They could be 'ome soon then, couldn't they? Per'aps I'd better not tell ma an' pa yet, they could be disappointed. What do yer think?"

Frank laughed. "I've never known you keep anything to yourself for long. But just warn them that it may be some while before the men return home."

It was three months before Arthur and William did arrive, but that was a noisy and joyful day. Almost the whole family arrived to greet them, filling the tiny cottage and spilling out into the garden.

They were welcomed as heroes, although no one really knew, or cared, what the outcome of the war had been.

Ann Newland's face beamed from one son to the other, and she kept touching first one and then the other as though to make sure they were really there.

James watched his mother, fascinated as usual by her capacity for love. He wondered if she was feeling, as he was now, that if only Ellen could be here, her family would be complete.

There had been very little news of her, except that someone returning home two years after she had gone had got word to them, saying that her baby Mary had died not long after their arrival in Tasmania, but Ellen had met and married someone else now and was reasonably content.

And Mary Ann, James thought—she should be here now, should be part of the family.

Later, when the crowd had thinned out and there was just James and his parents left sitting in the firelight with the two homecomers, Ann leaned forward and pulled Arthur's shirt away at the neck.

"Yer've lost an awful lot o' weight, son. I'll 'ave to feed yer up while yer 'ere."

John laughed. "Watch it son, yer'll be like a porker afore long."

The others joined in, but Arthur said soberly, "I've been a bit poorly ma, but I'll soon pick up now I'm 'ome."

"He was really ill at one time," William said. "I feared fer 'is life, but it were them women 'oo 'elped nurse 'im back."

"Women!" Ann was shocked, "What were women doin' out there, in a war?"

"They weren't near the fightin' ma, but they 'ad an 'ospital nearby, where they treated all the wounded soldiers." Arthur explained. "Took really good care of us they did, although how they coped with some o' the sights, I'll never know." He closed his eyes, as though to block out the horrors that he had seen.

William kicked a log back into the flames, which made the sap hiss and the smell of apple wood fill the room. "You've never seen anythin' like it, well, I 'ope yer never 'ave to. There were these women 'elpin' the doctors when they was sawin' off arms an' legs." He shuddered, in spite of the hot room.

"What made 'em even braver, "Arthur carried on, "was the fact that they 'ad to fight the authorities to go an' do it. Paid their own passage, some of 'em." He struggled with the emotion which threatened to overtake him. "Angels, we called 'em." It was a whisper, but a heartfelt one.

"Saw some pretty 'arrowin' sights then, son?" John asked, of no one in particular.

Both men nodded. "Well, yer know what it's like, pa, the battle-field." William said, "An' the trouble out there was that we didn't 'ave the right clothes nor nothin'. The uniforms was too thin and the food..." He shook his head and looked at Arthur. "No wonder 'e's so thin."

"Now, ma, don't you go upsettin' yerself," Arthur said, as Ann let out a sob.

"Why did yer 'ave to go? Why put up with all that terrible weather an' sickness an' sufferin', just for a scrap o' land not worth 'avin'?" she shouted. "Look at yer—yer 'ealth's ruined, an' fer what?"

There was a stunned silence, no one had ever heard her yell like that before.

Her husband went across the room to her in a single stride. "Shush, dear. Don't get so cross. It's 'ard to explain, but it's somethin' men do, fight wars. I know it weren't fer our own country, but we was 'elpin' sort out troubles..." He seemed at a loss to explain.

"Are yer goin' back to yer old jobs then?" James asked, to change the subject.

"I am," said William, "but Arthur's goin' to wait a while, 'til 'is 'ealth picks up."

"He can stay 'ere, I'll look after 'im myself." Their mother's firm voice, brooked no argument.

James was pleased that she would have someone to give her attention to—it seemed as though she needed it.

From then on, he hurried home each day to see how his brother was faring, and had a meal with him before going off to do someone's garden.

As the weeks turned into months and the onset of winter brought colder weather, it was obvious that Arthur was not getting any better. In fact he seemed to be wasting away before their very eyes and a hacking cough often left him too weak to move.

His mother had tried everything she could think of, all the broths and herbal teas, poultices and icy washes—nothing had any effect. Through the coldest part of the winter, James and his father gathered wood in every free hour to try and keep the cottage warm—but although the room would be stiflingly hot, Arthur would still sit and shiver.

No one expected him to live until the spring, but somehow he kept going. James had insisted on eating into his savings to pay for a doctor, but all the man could do was shake his head and say that it was the awful conditions in the Crimea that had brought on the illness. Apparently there were hundreds of men suffering in the same way. He gave Arthur some medicine to help with the pain and bring much needed sleep, but that was all.

On the warmer days, James would help his brother outside to sit in the sunshine.

"Yer know, James, this does make me feel a bit better, the fresh air and the warm sun. I just wish I could walk further." Arthur smiled. "You're not neglectin' yer gardenin' are yer, lookin' after me?"

"No, everyone understands," James replied lightly. He did not tell his brother that one or two folk had indeed felt let down, but most realised that his brother came first.

Frank Bates had been very understanding, even to letting him bring Solomon home to see if Arthur could sit on the horse and take a short ride. It had not been a success. Even with all his strength, it had taken James nearly half-an-hour to get his brother up into the saddle. And once this had been accomplished, he did not have the strength to hold himself upright, but kept sliding off to one side or the other.

Arthur had said he enjoyed seeing the horse anyway, and it was kind of Frank to offer.

The months drifted by and James fretted about Mary Ann as well as Arthur. He still prayed every night for her to come, and at just the glimpse of a slight figure in the distance his heart would miss a beat. But it was never her.

By late June, Arthur was confined to his bed. James spent as much time as he could with him. He would sit and recount all that had happened at the stables during the day, or regale him with local gossip, half of which was made-up, but at least it put a smile on Arthur's gaunt face. His body was nothing more than skin and bone now, and his breath came in short, wrenching rasps.

It was James, who shared the small upper room with his brother, who was bothered most by it. He would lie awake at night and listen to the laboured breathing, half afraid it would stop, but half hoping, for Arthur's sake, that it would.

One afternoon in July, James sat telling him of his day at work. "That Solomon, 'e don't arf sulk if Gretel's let out in the paddock afore 'im. 'E nearly kicked the door down t'day, an' she'd only been out fer five minutes. I'm sure that if they was 'umans they'd be man an' wife. Course, 'e's gelded so 'e ain't no use to 'er," he grinned at Arthur, "if yer knows what I mean."

The trace of a smile curved the thin lips. The doctor, who had called once a week and waived the fee, had just left, declaring to John and Ann that he marvelled at the man's resilience. They all knew that he was near the end, but tried to remain cheerful for his sake.

The day was searingly hot, and Arthur was propped up so that he could see out of the tiny window. "We need some rain, don't we? The ground's dry as a bone."

James had to lean forward to hear the words and then nodded in reply. "Don't look like we'll get any t'day though. It's a shame yer can't get down the stairs, it's cooler down there."

Arthur smiled a wan, sad smile. "I don't think I'll be goin' down again, do you?"

The hairs stood out on James' neck. "Oh, yer never know, yer might do it again one day."

But they both knew that he wouldn't.

Then suddenly Arthur said, "I think you've a visitor."

James thought he had misheard the words and leaned further forward, but Arthur forced his thin smile and pointed in the direction of the window.

At first James could see no one, and then a movement caught his eye. He peered out. His brother's eyesight must be better than his own, he decided, because it was several moments before he could see a slight figure walking up the lane towards the cottage.

And there in the shimmering heat, a small bag clasped in her hands, was Mary Ann.

Chapter Fifteen

Ann Newland looked up in surprise as her son hurled himself down the stairs, across the room and disappeared out of the door like the devil himself was at his back.

"Wha...?" She began, but he had gone.

He raced up the path calling her name, but stopped suddenly when he was within a few feet of her.

Mary Ann. She looked so beautiful, with the sunlight bringing an auburn sheen to her dark curls and showing off her figure in the flimsy material of her dress.

Shyness overcame him. "Is it really you?" he asked, feeling stupid, but unable to believe the proof of his own eyes.

She laughed, "Yes, it's really me." She held out her hand and he took it in his. He raised it to his lips and they stood, their eyes locked in wonder, for several moments. Then he wrapped his arms around her and held her close, vowing that no-one and nothing, would ever part them again.

"Yer've no idea, 'ow long I've waited fer this day, Mary Ann." He stood back a little and studied her. "Yer've grown even more lovely."

"Thank you, kind sir." She laughed again. "You look a little older, yourself. I've longed for it too, there were so many times when I thought I'd never get away. It's been difficult," she said more soberly.

"Oh, my poor love, there's never been a day when I ain't thought 'bout yer an' wished to be with yer. I wanted to come an' find yer, but didn't know where to start lookin'." It sounded weak to his own ears, but she smiled.

"I doubt you'd ever have found us. Mother kept us on the move, first the south coast, then London, then East Anglia." She shivered, in spite of the heat. "It was bitterly cold there."

"Oh, Mary Ann." James put his arm around her shoulders and led her back towards the cottage. "I'll bet yer could do with a drink, couldn't yer?"

"Yes, I've just walked from Greatham."

107

His mother had stood in the doorway watching, and now came forward. "'Ello, lass, it's good to see yer again. Come in and sit yer down."

Mary Ann smiled shyly and stepped into the welcoming cottage. And as she sat at the scrubbed wooden table, James was acutely aware that she was probably used to a better way of life. As though sensing his discomfort, she looked around the room and declared, "This is nice, I feel so much better now." She looked at Ann, "May I stay?"

"Of 'course yer can. We'll be 'appy to 'ave yer. Just rest awhile an' I'll get somethin' cool to drink."

James sat close by as Mary Ann drank thirstily from a cup of fruit juice. He could not take his eyes from her face, could not believe that she was actually here. His heart was full to overflowing with love and the knowledge that they need never be apart ever again. He wondered once more at his good fortune in having someone like her to love him as much as he loved her.

Later, when she was refreshed and rested, he took her up to meet Arthur. He was pleased to see her and made an effort to talk for a while, but soon he was unable to make himself heard and they left him to rest, but not before James saw the look of approval on his brother's face, accompanied by the merest hint of a wink.

After supper, she started to tell James and his parents of her life over the past few years and how she managed, at last, to get to Selborne.

She was still shy and not used to talking openly. James suspected that, in spite of everything, she was trying not to be disloyal to her mother.

"Losing grandmother so suddenly was horrible. Mother told me that she had sent word to Selborne and I couldn't understand why no one came to the funeral. I was so sad, but mother made out that people didn't care. I was sure she was wrong..." She brushed away a tear with the back of her hand and shook her head sorrowfully. "Then she insisted we go away and wouldn't tell anyone where we were going. She was so bitter, seemed to think everyone was against us." Desolation clouded her eyes. "She even hit me."

A ripple of disbelief went round the room, and James clenched his fists. "What for?" he demanded, certain that Mary Ann would never do anything to deserve that.

"I tried to make friends with a young couple who came from London. We were staying in a small hotel in Brighton and I thought that perhaps they would help me get away, but before I had a chance to speak to them mother realised what I was up to." She let out a long shuddering sigh. "She was very angry. I wasn't allowed out for a week after that, and by then the couple had left. Not long afterwards mother and I moved to London to see my father. I think our money was running out and she wanted to move on somewhere else. He must have given her something, because the next thing I knew we were on a coach to Great Yarmouth.

Ann Newland leaned forward and patted her hand. "You poor thing, 'ow long did yer stay there?"

"Months, all through the winter. We stayed in an awful place and the cold wind seemed to blow in through every gap. It was rather a run-down boarding house, but mother still didn't have enough to keep us there for long. Then it was back to London."

"Where did yer stay there, then?" asked John.

"My mother has an old school friend and we used to stay with her, but she and mother used to end up having arguments about me." Mary Ann shook her head, "But although she didn't approve, Aunt Tess wouldn't do anything to help me."

"Tch, tch, what a shame," Ann said.

"Mother took me along several times to see my father, but he was never interested in me—although they did have an argument one day because he didn't like the way she spoke to me. She ended up saying that he could look after me himself if he was so bothered. I couldn't believe that they could be so horrible in front of me." Her eyes filled with tears and James put an arm protectively around her.

"'Ow could they treat yer so? It don't make sense. They ought to be glad to 'ave a girl like you." He said fiercely.

"That they did." Put in John. "Some people…"

"Father told mother that she was not getting any more money from him and would have to sell the cottage in Froyle to pay for our keep." Her eyes grew large as she recounted what happened next. "There was an almighty row, because mother had to admit that she had already sold it. She had no right to do that, he said, and I thought he was going to hit her. He said some awful things. I just wanted to die." The tears came flooding at the memories.

"I think that's enough for now," John Newland said. "Time we was turnin' in. Mary Ann is exhausted, she needs 'er sleep." He rose from his seat. "Upstairs with yer, son—yer've work in the mornin'."

James reluctantly got to his feet. He didn't want to leave her for even a second, but he knew that his father was right.

"G'night Mary Ann, see yer in the mornin'" He bent and kissed her cheek tenderly.

"Night James." She replied shyly.

James climbed into his bed and lay for a while reliving the feel of her slender body in his arms and soft skin of her cheek beneath his lips.

And now she was here, she was here to stay.

He couldn't wait to finish work the next day and get home to see her, half afraid that she might have been spirited away.

Her face lit up at the sight of him. "Hello, dear James."

"'Ello, love, 'ow 'ave yer been today?"

"I'm fine now I've rested. I've been helping your ma a little with some of the mending. Look," she said, holding up one of his shirts, which sported a perfectly turned collar.

"She's a dab-hand at sewin', son—there's some lovely stitch-work there."

Mary Ann blushed at the unaccustomed praise and James beamed in pleasure.

After supper, with a little gentle encouragement, Mary Ann told them some more of her story. "I'm sorry I got upset last night."

"Don't apologise," John told her softly, "yer'd every right to be upset."

She smiled warmly at the kind words. "I still find it strange not to have every word I say either ignored or dismissed."

"'Ow yer put up with it all that time, I'll never know." Ann sighed.

" I didn't know how to get away, I had no money and no one to help me. While we were in London I kept a look out for the couple from Brighton, but I never saw them—it's such a big place." She took a deep breath, determined to tell them the rest. "Time dragged on at aunt Tess's house, but I could see that she didn't really want us there. I don't think mother was paying her for our keep. In the end she insisted we had to go, so mother went to visit father again. He was adamant that she was not getting any more money out of him. He had bought one home and as far as he was concerned he had done his duty. He didn't want to have any more to do with us." She looked around the friendly faces. "I honestly thought that we would end up living on the streets, but in the end father said that he would arrange for us to stay at his father's house, just until I was twenty-one." Her face lit up. "I was pleased with that idea because grandfather lives at

Greatham now and I thought that I could get from there to here quite easily. My birthday was only two months away so I knew it wouldn't be for long."

"But yer birthday were last October, what 'appened?" James butted in.

"Give the girl a chance, don't rush 'er." His father scolded gently.

Her face clouded. "When we arrived, grandfather made it perfectly clear to mother that it was only a short term arrangement. Although he has a very large house and there would have been plenty of room, I suppose he didn't think it his duty to keep us. He was pleasant to me and I thought that he might understand, so I told him about you, James." She stopped and hesitated.

"What did 'e say to that news?" he asked, guessing the answer.

"He got very cross and told me that I was an ungrateful girl wanting to marry a common labourer after all he had done for me. I tried to explain, tried to make him understand, but he wouldn't listen." She shook her head. "It seemed so unfair. He had a terrible row with mother, saying that it was all her fault because she had trapped his son into marriage, and that he only had her word for the fact that I was really his granddaughter." Tears filled her eyes. "It was horrible. I tried to run away then, but he sent one of his men out to take me back." Mary Ann started to tremble. "And then I was locked in my room."

"What! kept a prisoner ... like a common thief." John Newland said, a look of horror on his face.

"If only I'd known." James was distraught. "Oh, my poor love. To think yer was so close, an' I didn't know, couldn't 'elp." He threw his hands up.

"The wicked old man, 'e'd no right to take 'is son's wrong-doings out on you," Ann added to the general feeling of disgust.

They sat quietly for a while as James held the sobbing Mary Ann in the crook of his arm and kissed her forehead gently. "Yer'll never get treated like that ever again, I promise yer, not while there's breath in me body," he murmured.

"You weren't locked up all this time, was yer?" John asked.

Mary Ann shook her head. "No. About a week after all this happened, grandfather was taken ill, a stroke I think the doctor said. He was very poorly for a long time and mother looked after him in return for our keep. She made me help as well, but she still wouldn't let me out, not even to walk around the gardens. I used to sit with grandfather at night sometimes, but he wouldn't speak to me. I used to sit and work out plans to get away, but before I could try any of them I got sick." She smiled at James, "Oh, it wasn't that serious, but I was in bed for two weeks and it was then that I made friends with one of the maids. She took pity on me when she heard what had happened and decided that once I was well enough she would help me get away."

John got up to tap his pipe out on the fireplace. "I think your ma 'as a lot to answer for." He said sternly.

Mary Ann nodded sadly and bit her lip.

"So this maid 'elped yer get out, did she?" James, as usual, was impatient to know every detail.

"Give 'er a chance son," John said firmly, "It's painful for 'er, tellin' us all this. Mind you, once it's told, that'll be an end to it. There'll be no more said to anyone, not even the family, otherwise them girls of our'n will 'ave spread all sorts round the village, an' we don't want that."

"Thank you Mr Newland, I think that would be best." Mary Ann gave him one of her lovely smiles.

"Do yer think anyone'll come lookin' for yer?" James asked.

"I doubt it, or they'd probably have been here by now. I expect they're glad to see the back of me."

James stroked her hand. "They must be mad, that's all I can say. Now, 'ow did yer get out?"

"Well, Sarah, that was her name, knew that after lunch on a Sunday both the cook and the housekeeper went to lie down, so that meant that the kitchen area was empty. Before I caught my heavy cold I'd had to share a room with my mother, so that she could keep watch on me, but then because she didn't want to get ill as well, I was moved to a room of my own." She smiled wanly. "It was little more than a box-room really, but at least I had some time to myself. Sarah and I decided to put our plan into action quickly in case mother wanted me back with her." Her light, vivacious laugh filled the room. "I did enjoy the adventure of getting away. To be honest, I didn't think of any consequences—I just couldn't wait to leave that house. Sarah came to my room as soon as all was quiet and smuggled me down the back stairs, across the kitchen and out of the backdoor. I ran to some nearby shrubs and then made my way towards the road. I asked directions from a woman ... and here I am." Mary Ann finished, obviously tired, but also, James was sure, relieved.

"Well, yer safe 'ere now with us, lass. Yer need rest an' feedin' 'til yer get yer strength back. An' we'll be pleased to think of yer as one o' the family. Now I've got yer bed ready so I think yer'd better be off to it." Ann Newland showed her pleasure and affection by kissing the girl on the cheek, which made Mary Ann blush and brought tears to her eyes again. But at least they were tears of happiness.

John nodded his agreement. "We ain't got much, but yer welcome to share what we 'ave."

"Well, we don't go 'ungry do we ma?" James pulled Mary Ann to her feet. "Ma's right, time fer yer bed."

Ann gave her a candle to see her way and she walked up the rough stairway, so very different to what she was used to, and turned at the top of them. "I'll never be able to thank you enough. I feel at home here already."

"That's thanks enough in itself, lass."

James could have sworn that he saw his father wipe a tear from the corner of his eye.

113

Chapter Sixteen

James sat quietly by his brother's bedside and listened, with some amusement, to the voices in the kitchen below, where his mother was showing Mary Ann how to make bread.

The girl's merry laugh floated upward on the still air. It was a hot day and the sun's rays glanced in under the thatched roof to highlight the dancing motes of dust and make a pool of light on the bare boards.

Arthur was now so weak that he could barely move or speak and over the past few days those of his brothers and sisters who lived near enough had visited him to say their silent farewells.

James studied the skeletal figure lying in the bed. Arthur was still a young man, but his chance of living a long and happy life had been lost on that faraway battlefield, and to his grieving family it was a terrible waste.

As the sun shifted round the sky, the pool of sunlight became smaller and James watched in fascination until it disappeared altogether, and as he watched he dreamed about the day when he could take Mary Ann as his wife. He would ask Mr Wright about a cottage and there would be a lovely family wedding, and then they would settle down and have lots of children…

He must have dozed, because he awoke suddenly to find the room in shadow. The smell of baking bread wafted in through the open doorway and he decided go and see what success Mary Ann had had at her first attempt.

But as he rose from the chair, he suddenly realised how quiet it was. The silence was palpable and his scalp prickled as he looked down at his brother. The laboured breathing had stopped and Arthur's last battle was over.

James trod quietly down the stairs. The look on his face must have told its own story, because as his mother saw him she raised a hand to her mouth and closed her eyes.

"He's gone?" The whispered question hung in the air.

"Yes, ma. It were very peaceful." James crossed the room to take her hands and lead her to a chair.

"I'm alright son, I've been expecting it for days." She bit her lip and whispered as much to herself as to anyone else. "My dear Arthur. God bless you, son."

"I'll go an' fetch pa, shall I?" James offered.

His mother nodded as Mary Ann sat down beside her and put a comforting arm round her shoulders.

William had wanted to make the funeral a military affair, but Ann was determined that it was to be a quiet family occasion.

When it was all over and everyone had gone home, James and Mary Ann left the cottage for a walk together.

James was pensive. "I think ma an' pa need some time to 'emselves. It's been 'orrible for 'em, losin' Arthur like that."

Mary Ann put her hand in his and smiled. "I liked him you know, in the short time that I knew him. I found some of the qualities I admire in you in him as well."

It was a beautiful evening and the warm air brought out the scent of honeysuckle and wild roses as they strolled along the pathway above the cottage. The sky was alive with darting swallows and late butterflies still searched among the flowers for nectar.

James smiled contentedly, the sadness for his brother eased a little by being in the company of the girl he loved.

They still found a multitude of things to talk about, what they had done and seen over the years. James especially loved to hear about Brighton and resolved that they would go there together one day. To him it sounded like another world and try as she might, Mary Ann couldn't convince him that the sea was so vast. She laughed and gave up in desperation when he said that he could not picture it at all—she must be making it up.

Soon, they found themselves at the foot of the steep hanger that enclosed the village. "It looks 'igh," said James, "but there's an easy way up there—the zig-zag path."

"It might be easy to you, you don't have to wear skirts," she teased.

"Good job an' all. Do yer want to go up the path? The view's lovely from the top."

"All right, but we shouldn't really go on our own, should we?" Mary Ann said. "We haven't got a chaperone."

"We ain't in London now," he reasoned. "There's no place for the likes o' that 'ere."

"Right, I'll race you to the top." And off she sped, dashing along each pathway with surprising speed, skirts held up to her knees in a most unladylike fashion, much to James' delight.

They reached the grassy bank at the top together and flopped, laughing, on the ground to catch their breath and admire the panorama below.

"It's well worth the climb, James—you're right. How far can you see?"

He shrugged, "Dunno, a few miles I 'spose."

"Oh, look you can see the church, doesn't it look tiny? And the houses, they're like toys." She sighed. "I want to stay here for ever."

"Gets a bit chilly at night." He grinned wickedly.

Mary Ann slapped him on the arm playfully. "In Selborne, I meant."

He took her hand gently, and said seriously, "If yer marry me, yer can stay 'ere fer the rest o' yer life."

Her face lit up and she squeezed his hand. "I'd like nothing better."

"We'll just give ma and pa a while to get over losin' Arthur, then we'll arrange a weddin', right?" He put his arm around her shoulders and they sat in quiet companionship, content in each others company and in a world of their very own.

After a while he pulled her to her feet. "We'll just walk a little way along the top path, then we'll start back."

She gazed at the massive beech and oak trees along the way and picked a bunch of wild campion, pink and white. Then suddenly she led the way under the low branches of a beech tree which opened up into a vast space around the tree-trunk, and let out a slow breath, staring upwards in wonder. "It's like a cathedral."

James, who had never seen a cathedral in his life, felt at something of a disadvantage, but had to agree that the effect was amazing. It was cool and dim under the canopy where the sunlight barely penetrated, and it was eerily quiet.

Mary Ann shivered and moved closer to James. He put his arms around her, tenderly at first, but then the warmth of her body through the fine material of her dress caught him unawares.

He looked down into her eyes and saw love and trust there, and something else; she was feeling the same. "I love yer Mary Ann. I love yer so much." Passion coursed through his body, but he pulled away.

"I love you too. I've waited for so long, please hold me."

He struggled for breath. "No, I'll do somethin' I shouldn't..."

But she put her arms around him and held him tight, lifting her mouth to his.

He kissed her soft pink lips, surprised at the eager response, but thrilling in it. He caressed her body gently at first, but then with a mounting fever, until he heard her draw in a deep shuddering breath.

"James, oh, James." She murmured huskily.

Then he knew that there could be no turning back. They were both consumed with desire, both committed to the final act of love—they belonged together, and all the years of pain and separation dissolved into the balmy air around them.

The pair remained locked in their own little heaven, until James suddenly realised that it was almost dark outside. Reluctantly they walked back down the hill, arms around each other, stopping to kiss often, until the cottage came into view. Only then did they release their hold.

"You all right, lass?" Ann Newland asked Mary Ann, who nodded and moved away from the doorway, still shivering.

"I just needed some fresh air, I'll be fine." She sat at the table and picked up the mug of hot tea.

"I 'spect this place is not quite what you're used to—it's not so cosy in winter," John said, pulling on his jacket. "I'll be gettin' off then."

A blast of cold air filled the room as he closed the door behind him and Mary Ann shivered again. "I'll have to make myself a thicker shawl, I don't know why I'm feeling so cold."

Just then, James came clattering down the stairs. "'Ow's my two favourite girls this mornin' then?" He sat next to Mary Ann and kissed her on the cheek, then pulled back and looked at her more closely. "Are yer alright, love? Yer look a bit pale an' yer face is cold."

He glanced at his mother who, far from looking worried, smiled—then back at Mary Ann, now holding the mug of tea between both hands and sipping slowly. Her large blue eyes gazed back at him. "I'm just feeling the cold, that's all."

Ann sat down on the opposite bench and considered each of them in turn. "There's no other way of puttin' this, but is it possible yer with child?"

Mary Ann blushed to her roots. It was James who turned pale now.

"'Cos if yer are, then we better start arrangin' a weddin'." Ann seemed not at all worried about the possibilities.

Mary Ann turned to James and dropped her gaze demurely. She bit her lip, "Do you think I might be?"

James saw his mother clamp a hand over her mouth to stop the laughter which was apparent in her eyes. He didn't know what to say, but remembered the many warm, sunny evenings that he and Mary Ann had spent in wonderful togetherness.

"I-I, er, 'spose." Was all he could manage.

"Yer'd best get down to see the vicar then, son. Don't worry lass, yer not the first, an' yer won't be the last." She patted her small white hand. "We'll 'ave a Christmas weddin'—that'll be nice."

But the next day, James arrived home with a glum expression after seeing the vicar. "'E can't marry us afore Christmas, I'm afraid. Will New Year's Day suit?"

Mary Ann beamed and threw her arms around him. His mother and father both said that it would be fine and there was a general round of hugs and hand shakes.

From then on James could talk about nothing else, which caused Mary Ann much amusement. "I thought that I should be the one to be most excited," She told Eliza, who was visiting with Harriet to help choose what to wear and what flowers to carry.

"It's so difficult this time of year—there's not much about in the way of flowers," said Harriet.

"We could have holly and Ivy decorating the church," said Mary Ann, who had seen this at a church in London.

"Oooh, that sounds lovely," Eliza enthused. "We'll go down the day afore an' put up as much as we can find, I'm sure the vicar won't mind."

"And I would like to carry my prayer book, the one grandmother gave me." Mary Ann stood patiently as her favourite blue dress was pulled and tweaked down over her figure. "I've filled out a bit since I've been here, must be your mother's cooking."

Eliza and Harriet grinned knowingly. "That must be it," they agreed.

Christmas came and went almost unnoticed in the run-up to the wedding. Members of the family, some of whom Mary Ann had never met before, arrived with gifts and best wishes, and an assurance of being there on the day. James asked William to stand up with him in church. An offer which was accepted and proudly related to anyone who had the time to listen.

The only thing which bothered James was Mary Ann's health. She was very pale and he knew that she had been sick on several occasions. He voiced his concern to his mother, but she reassured him that this was normal. He was still worried though, and one evening when they were on their own he told her so.

"I do feel a little weak, but I'll be alright, you'll see." She gave him a bright smile. "It's early days yet." And with that he had to be content.

In the days before the wedding, Ann, Mary Ann, Eliza and Harriet spent hours cooking. There was fresh bread and a fruit cake, roasted chickens, a goose and a joint of pork, and a selection of fruit pies just for good measure.

Mr Wright had sent the pork with his best wishes, a kind gesture which the whole family appreciated. "It'll make a nice change to 'ave a bit o' porker," John had enthused.

"Tastier than rabbit any day," James said, although he was so excited that he didn't feel he would be able to eat anything.

The kitchen was filled with animated voices and tantalising smells, while the menfolk kept themselves busy sorting out homemade ale and fruit cordials, and discussing the various merits— or otherwise—of married life.

On New Year's Eve, when all was done that could be, Harriet and Eliza set off, weary but cheerful, for their homes. It was almost dark and it was starting to snow.

"Oh, a real white weddin'," Ann said with a wink at Mary Ann, who blushed again at the thought of her condition.

"The snow won't get too deep, will it?" she asked hurriedly.

"Shouldn't think so, lass, we don't usually get it too bad 'ere." John reassured her.

"I'll carry yer there if I 'ave to," James laughed. "Yer ain't gettin' away from me now."

They settled down for a quiet evening in the candlelit kitchen, Mary Ann reading from her prayer book and Ann sewing on a last minute button, while James and his father talked about work and the weather.

After a while, Ann looked up. "You look tired lass, it's time for yer bed—it'll be a long day tomorrer." She smiled in concern. "An' yer'll strain yer eyes readin' by that light." Then she rose from her seat and went into the next room, returning with a package. "But 'old on a minute—it's goin' to be cold in that church, so I'd like yer to 'ave this."

Gently, Mary Ann pulled away a swathe of thin paper to reveal a shawl. It was made of thick, soft wool, knitted in an intricate pattern of pale blue and white. She lifted it out and held the softness to her face. It smelled faintly of lavender, and she let out a long sigh. Then smiling up at Ann she said, "It's beautiful, thank you so much. I'll be proud to wear it. It goes with my dress too." And putting the shawl around her shoulders, she hugged it under her chin.

"My mother made it for my weddin'," said Ann, "but I've never passed it on to any o' my girls 'cos, to be 'onest, they don't look after things—but I think yer will."

"Oh, I will, I'll treasure it. Isn't it lovely, James?"

"It is, an' it suits yer too," he said proudly.

"I'll never be able to thank you enough—for everything, I mean. I've been made so welcome by everyone, and Harriet and Eliza have treated me just like a real sister." A tear came to her eye. "You've all been so kind."

James moved to her side. "Don't upset yerself, dear. Ma's right— yer tired, so off yer go. See yer in the mornin'." He kissed her cheek and held her for a moment before she said goodnight and climbed the stairs to the room above.

"We'll take that curtain down in the mornin' eh ma?"

His mother chuckled. "Yes, we certainly will." The curtain was the one Ann and John had insisted was put up to divide the upper room into two, as it had been when the girls were all at home, to give Mary Ann some privacy. Tomorrow it would come down and the two beds would be pushed together for the couple to start their married life.

James went hot around the collar when he thought of what had happened. He hadn't meant to get Mary Ann with child before they were married—it just didn't occur to either of them that it might happen—but nonetheless, those wonderful evenings up on the hanger would live in his heart until his dying day.

A little later he went up to bed himself, and had to fight the temptation to peep around the curtain to see if Mary Ann was asleep. Tomorrow night she would be with him, and they would enjoy many more nights as they lived out the rest of their lives together.

John Newland knocked his pipe out on the hearth. "Well, I'm turnin' in." He went to peer out of the window. "There's still a fair bit fallin'"

Ann looked up. "What, the snow? Is it thick?"

"Job to see." He crossed to the door and opened it. The dim light from inside the kitchen showed that the ground was well covered. "Should be alright, long as it don't snow all night." He said.

Ann packed away her sewing. "Well, we'll 'ave to 'ope for the best, but it's goin' to be cold in that church anyway."

The following morning the world had been transformed. Snow had fallen heavily all night and was now many feet deep.

"I've never seen anythin' like this. Not in all my years," John said in amazement.

Mary Ann was fighting back tears. "Why, oh why, did this have to happen, today of all days. Is there no way we can get to the church?" She knew what the answer would be.

John peered through the top two inches of window. "Sorry, lass. Look, it's over the tops of the 'edge, an' yer can't see where the lane is s'posed to be. We wouldn't make it more than a few yards." They couldn't even open the door—James had tried, but a wall of snow had fallen inside and taken him and his father the best part of an hour to clear, and they'd only managed that by carrying it upstairs in a bucket and throwing it out of the bedroom window.

James had tried to keep cheerful at first for Mary Ann's sake, but gradually as the day wore on with no sign of a let-up in the snow fall, he despaired with her.

"At least we've plenty to eat." Ann tried to sound jolly, but it landed on deaf ears and the four of them sat around in gloomy silence.

John puffed on an empty pipe and stared into the fire. "Good job we brought in all these logs yesterday."

James and Mary Ann couldn't settle. First one, then the other would go to the tiny patch of window to see if the snow had stopped, or if there was a hint of blue sky appearing anywhere.

By evening the snow still fell thick and fast, and the temperature dropped alarmingly with the darkness.

"There's nothin' for it," said Ann, "we'll 'ave to go to bed to keep warm so's we can save what wood we 'ave. Never mind, per'aps it'll be better tomorrer."

Then James came to a decision. "I'm puttin' the beds together, sorry ma, but Mary Ann'll freeze to death on 'er own."

"That's alright son, I was goin' to suggest it anyway."

And so he settled down for the night next to his bride-to-be. "Don't worry dear, it can't last fer ever," he whispered, then sighed

121

deeply. "Still, it weren't the sort o' weddin' day we'd 'oped fer, was it?"

The fierce weather held its grip all through the next few days. No word could be got in or out, and Ann Newland fretted about the rest of the family.

John and James battled through the drifts to work each day, but once there they found little could be done except to give the animals feed and keep their living quarters clean. The cows still had to be milked, and as the wagon could not get through to collect it, the men were each allowed to take some home—a life-saver for many.

In the Newland household, the situation was getting grimmer by the day. The food prepared for the wedding soon dwindled down to nothing, the flour bin was all but empty, and there was very little wood for the fire.

One day James struggled for hours to dig out some logs from the pile in the garden. They were wet through, so he put most in the shed to dry, and the bit he brought indoors spat out sap and smoked.

He also had the unhappy task of telling his father that all his chickens were either dead or missing.

"Poor things, must've frozen to death. They ain't no good for eatin' I 'spose?"

"Nah, some'ow a fox 'as got to 'em—there ain't much left." He looked sorrowfully out of the window, "Shouldn't think much 'as survived this lot, not even the foxes."

Early in January they moved all the beds into the kitchen and slept in their clothes, putting on as many layers as possible. Everything from old curtains, sheets and even spare petticoats were piled on to cover them at night, and James and his father had nailed a piece of wood across the window hoping that it would do a better job of keeping the cold out there than it would of giving any lasting heat on the fire.

One morning, when James managed to dig his way down the lane and into the village after another heavy snowfall, he was glad to find that the previous day a wagon had arrived from Alton and there were a few provisions on sale in the shop. He brought back with him a small sack of barley, a two pound bag of flour and three small turnips.

He had also been given the news that the vicar was ill.

"What's wrong with 'im then?" asked his mother.

"Dunno, they didn't say."

Mary Ann sighed, "Poor man. I hope he gets better soon, then if the thaw starts we can get to the church."

James put his arm around her, "We'll just 'ave to 'ope dear. Sorry there ain't more to eat. I'll try an' dig out some o' them early 'taters."

"They won't be ready, son," John said. "They'll need weeks yet. There's none left in the shed, I 'spose?"

"I thought yer brought 'em all in, but I'll go an' 'ave a look."

James stepped inside the shed, gripping the door-jamb for support. The stone flagons of ale had broken, spilt over the floor and frozen.

"What a waste," John had grumbled when he heard.

James peered around the shed's dim interior. There were still some logs left drying out, but very little else. Then he noticed a small sack laying in a corner. It was wet to the touch and stuck to the ale-covered floor, but when he pulled it away and looked inside he saw it was half-full of oatmeal.

He hurried back indoors, pleased with his find, and to his amazement his mother started to laugh heartily when he showed her. "We'll all get drunk eating that," she hooted.

Soon, they all joined in, laughing until their sides ached, the merriment releasing some of the tension. John stoked the fire, Ann made a hot drink, and the oatmeal bubbled with one of the turnips in a saucepan. The smell of it reminded James of chicken mash, but he was so hungry it didn't seem to matter.

Weeks passed without any real sign of a thaw and Mary Ann's condition continued to worry James. She was pale and gaunt, and very quiet. She should have been blooming by now, he thought.

"What can I do, ma?" He asked helplessly.

Ann sat and shook her head sadly. "I wish I knew, son. She needs feedin', but…"

Even with meagre rationing, all the oatmeal, barley and flour had gone, and still the vice-like freeze carried on. There had been no more deliveries to Selborne, food could not be bought and most of the villagers were suffering.

James knew that if he was to save the lives of both his wife and unborn child, he had to do something quickly.

"Are yer sure them taters won't be ready, yet?" he asked his father.

"Even if they were, you'd never get a fork into the soil."

"Can I try?"

"Well, it's up to yer, but I don't 'old out much 'ope."

James fetched the garden fork from the shed and set to work in the potato patch. Time after time he tried to force the tool into the soil, but his father had been right, it was solid.

He tried further along the row. No good. Another row, still nothing. Frustration and anger built up inside him, giving force to his thrust with the fork. Row after row he tried, but to no avail. He stopped near the chicken coop to rest for a moment, wiping the sweat from his brow. His breath formed a white cloud in the frosty air and he looked up as his father came up to him.

"No luck, son?"

"It's useless, pa, just like yer said it would be. I don't know what to do. Mary Ann is sufferin' 'cos of me." He flung the fork down in desperation.

He and John looked down in amazement as it stuck in the ground at their feet. James grasped the handle and worked it backwards and forwards.

"Look pa, the ground's softer 'ere. The 'edge must give it a bit of shelter. It's carrots 'ere ain't it?"

"Yeh, but I doubt they're any good yet. Go on let's see."

James started to dig and after the first few forkfuls one tiny red-pink carrot appeared. He carried on with renewed vigour and was rewarded with several more. His father stooped to pick them up and carried them in his hands as though they were gold bars.

"Carry on, son." He said excitedly, "There must be a few more."

After what seemed like an age they had enough for a meal, albeit a small one.

"I'll try again tomorrer," said James, looking down at his blistered hands. "We might even get some o' the taters."

His father smiled and James noticed how haggard and grey he was —the harsh winter had certainly taken its toll.

Ann pulled a face when she saw the carrots. "We'll 'ave to expect a bit of a belly ache—frosted veg does that. Still, that's all there is. Well done, son"

So that night, they sat at the table with a small plate of carrots each. "Nice, ain't they?" said James with a sardonic grin, and somehow everyone managed to laugh.

The following day though, they really did have a feast. A neighbour knocked on the door to tell Ann that a carter had arrived from Alton, and he was loaded with food and other essentials.

She hurried down to the shop and found that almost everyone else was there. The shopkeeper and the carter were selling goods straight off the back of the wagon, such was the demand.

Ann bought as much as her money would allow and found, much to her relief, that James had turned up to help her carry it.

"Oh, son, thank goodness you're 'ere. I'd never 'ave managed this on me own."

He grinned, "Blimey ma, yer makin' up fer lost time, ain't yer." But they went home with happy hearts.

To add to their good fortune, Mr Wright had arrived home from abroad and, appalled at the plight of his employees, had given the farm manager instructions to slaughter enough chickens to give them one each. John arrived home triumphant with his and they all eyed the bird hungrily.

"Mary Ann will get a decent meal at last," said James.

Ann Newland cried with gratitude when she saw it, and when John said that there would be a joint of pork for them the following day, she was overcome with weeping. James realised what a strain she had been under, trying to eke out meals from practically nothing all the long weeks.

While the chicken was cooking, James and his father went out into the garden and dug a few more carrots. Then they tried the potatoes again. This time they dug in the nearest patch to the hedgerow. Success! There were only a few and they were still small, but it made an addition to the meal.

Gradually the thaw set in, slowly at first, but by the third week in February the snow had all but gone and life could return to normal.

"I'll go to see vicar tomorrer," James told Mary Ann happily. "We can be married at last."

Chapter Seventeen

Mary Ann eased herself into the wooden armchair, one hand on her back.

"Is it achin'?" asked Harriet, and then added knowingly, "it does towards the end. Still, never mind, not long now. Once we get today over..."

Mary Ann grimaced. "A fine bride I'm going to look."

Eliza bustled into the tiny kitchen with some flowers she had gathered from the hedgerow along the lane.

"Oh, they're lovely, thank you. They'll hide my belly a little." She took the little bouquet and admired the blooms. Creamy-white wild roses with a blush of pink, sweet-scented lily-of-the-valley and a few blue-purple columbines were cleverly arranged, the stems bound together with a piece of blue ribbon. "Where did you get that?" she asked pointing to the ribbon.

"That would be tellin'," Eliza winked. "I thought as they would be enough, as yer carryin' yer prayer book."

Mary Ann nodded. "Just right."

It was May and the baby was due in four weeks time—and she and James were only just getting married. Sometimes she had despaired of it ever happening at all. The past three months had been long and arduous, with first one thing and then another going wrong every time they made arrangements.

The vicar's wife had been most apologetic, but he had to go away to convalesce after being ill for most of the winter. The man sent to stand in had been called away on family business and then, when they had decided to get married in Alton, the vicar there had so many weddings and christenings to do—due to the long cold spell he said—that it had been quicker to await the return of their own after all.

And at last the day arrived, the sun shone, and she had Harriet and Eliza clucking around her like two mother hens.

They had helped her let out the seams on her dress still further, and given much advice on motherhood, which Ann had told her to take with a pinch of salt.

"I'll see yer alright, dear," she had said. "Them two girls get a mite carried away."

Mary Ann stood up to put her bonnet on and Harriet placed one of the sprigs of lily-of-the-valley into the blue ribbon around the brim. "There, yer look a picture, don't she Lizzie?"

"Real pretty," Eliza said, tweaking a few tendrils of hair out at the sides of the bonnet to frame Mary Ann's face. "There." She stood back to admire her handiwork. "Yer'll do."

"Thank you both for your help. I feel quite presentable now. I'll carry grandmother's prayer book with the flowers sprayed across it— it'll look rather nice."

"Are we all ready?" asked Ann as she entered from the bedroom. "My, yer look lovely, Mary Ann, yer really do."

"Coo, ma, yer look alright yerself," Eliza said. "They'll be wonderin' which one's the bride."

"Oh, you…" Ann flapped a hand at her.

As the women stepped out into the sunshine they were met by a crowd of excited neighbours. There were cheers all round as James appeared—together with William—and stood with a look of love and admiration shining from his eyes at the sight of Mary Ann. He took her hand and whispered. "Shall we go."

She nodded, a wide smile lighting up her face. "My, James Newland," she teased, "you're looking very smart. I shall be pleased to walk down the street with you."

They set off along the lane at the head of a small group of friends and family, but as they proceeded more and more villagers joined the parade.

Some waved from their windows, others called out from their doorways wishing them good luck, and others threw flowers picked from their gardens onto the pathway, the crushed blooms sending up a rich and heady perfume.

By the time they reached the church, there seemed to be nearly half the village behind them.

The vicar welcomed them with a smile and waited patiently while everyone squeezed into the church. A hush had descended over the congregation before he began, "Dearly beloved, we are gathered here…"

To James, the service passed in a haze. The bright sunlight pouring through the windows reminded him of another, sadder day and he wondered with a sudden pang if Tom was somehow there, and as his arm brushed that of his beloved Mary Ann standing at his side, he was filled with such emotion that he thought his heart would burst.

At last she was his, they were man and wife and he walked proudly down the aisle with her on his arm, smiling joyfully at those filling the pews on either side. He turned his head again to look at her and marvelled once more at her beauty, and the fact that she loved him. He knew that he was the luckiest man in the whole world.

As they emerged through the porchway, they saw that Frank Bates and the stable lads were forming a double rank of cheering escorts, and then just outside the gate was another surprise. Standing under the oak tree in the Plestor stood Solomon and Gretel.

This was too much for James. He rushed over to where they stood, pulling Mary Ann behind him. Both horses looked up from cropping the grass and shivered as though sensing the excitement of the day. Snickering and snorting and looking for a tit-bit or apple which James would normally have for them, they allowed themselves to be patted and fussed. Then James noticed something else—to his amazement, sitting there with his pony and trap was Mr Wright, and he was holding out a piece of paper.

"Here you are, young man. This is the lease to the cottage next door to your parents. I hope that will be satisfactory." This was said rather formally, but once he had finished, he jumped down from the buggy and said, "Now I hope that I get to kiss the bride—you are a very lucky fellow by the looks of things." And to Mary Ann's surprise, and embarrassment, he kissed her boldly on the cheek.

James stammered his thanks. What a wedding gift, their very own cottage. He touched his forelock and bowed. "We're both thrilled, Mr Wright, sir. It's more than we could 'ave wished for."

"You are very welcome, Newland. You have been an excellent employee, both to me and for my predecessors. Many good wishes for your future." He climbed back into the trap and sat, smiling, to watch the wedding party move off along the street.

As they rejoined the milling throng, James clutched the paper to his chest. He couldn't wait to show his father and brothers. And the glowing words ... he hardly knew how to stop from crying. He just held Mary Ann against him and said, "We've got our own 'ome, dear. Think of it." He kissed her cheek. "We're goin' to be so 'appy, I just know it." Then he glanced up. "But I think we'd better get a move on now, or they'll maybe start the weddin' breakfast without us!"

And laughing, they ran along the street hand in hand.

Back at the cottage, Mary Ann was given a chair in the shade and told to rest quietly. She was then witness to the most amazing spectacle she had ever seen. In what seemed like no time at all the lawn was transformed as trestle tables were set up, chairs put around them and a mountain of food placed on top. It looked like the feast to end all feasts.

James came to stand beside her. "Looks like everyone's been cookin' fer weeks. Come to the table, we've got to be seated first."

Shyly, she walked across to where William was holding out a chair for her. He bowed very deeply in mock solemnity. "Madam."

She giggled and sat down, James beside her, and then everyone else scrambled to be next—all except John and Ann who sat either side of the bride and groom.

It was a merry meal, and although Mary Ann could not eat very much, she enjoyed what she managed. "I think I must be dreaming, isn't it marvellous?" she said to John. "Who did all this?"

"I think 'alf o' the village 'ad an 'and in it. I'm not sure 'oo set it all off though. What a spread! We 'ad nothin' like this when we was wed, did we mother?" He leaned forward and looked across at Ann.

"We certainly didn't, but I wasn't sure yer remembered back that far," she said with a wicked grin.

"Well, I do. I remember very well indeed." He then proceeded to regale them with a very humorous account of their wedding day, all those years before. Ann butted in from time to time to call him a fibber, but it made for an enjoyable and happy meal.

Somehow most of the food was eaten—and the ale drunk—and once the tables were all but empty, they were cleared away and the music began.

There was much clapping and singing to start with, and then a few couples started off the dancing. James held out his hand to Mary Ann.

"Just one then," she said. "I can't manage anything too energetic. It's so hot too, how can they do that?" She pointed to a couple performing a very lively jig.

A little later, after their more sedate effort, they wandered inside to rest in the quiet of the kitchen. "Well, Mrs Newland, 'ow does it feel to be a married woman?"

"I quite like it so far, but it's early days yet," she answered, trying, but failing, to keep a straight face. "Do you know what I really wish?"

"What's that?"

"That grandmother and grandfather could have been here. They would have enjoyed it so, and they'd have been very happy for us I know."

James took her hand. "It would 'ave been nice. Pity yer ma wouldn't come too."

Mary Ann bit her lip. "It's her decision—she can't say she wasn't asked, nor grandfather Knight."

At Ann's insistence an invitation had been extended to Charlotte Knight and her father-in-law, but as expected they had not even sent an answer.

A tear crept into the corner of Mary Ann's eye, but she brushed it away angrily. "I don't care, I don't owe her anything. She's not spoiling today for me. It's been magical—I never thought that so many people would be here and that we would have so much goodwill shown to us." Her face brightened. "And the cottage! I still think I'm dreaming."

"Tell yer what I could do, I could ask vicar to write somethin' in yer grandma's prayer book for yer."

"Oooh, yes! That sounds a lovely idea." She put her arms around him and kissed his cheek. "I like being Mrs Newland more with each passing minute." She got up and went to fetch her prayer book. "What are you going to ask him to write?"

He shrugged, "Dunno, I'll leave it up to 'im." And off he went.

Ann came in as James went out. "Is this where yer 'idin'. Mind it is cooler in 'ere." She sat down. "'Ow are yer feelin'?"

"Happy. Tired, but happy. No, that doesn't really explain how I feel, I'm so overcome with it all..." She smiled and sighed deeply. "I never knew people could be so kind. It has been the most marvellous day. And now James has taken my prayer book to the vicar to be written in."

"He's thoughtful, isn't he? He's always been the one to think of such things. I'm glad that 'e has you now—yer well suited." She leaned back and relaxed with her back against the wall. "It's all a mother can ask fer, that 'er children are 'appy."

"I'm glad we'll be living close. Aren't we lucky to get next door?" She look at Ann shyly. "Can I call you ma, like James does?"

"'Course yer can, dear. I'd like that."

"I feel that for the first time in my life I have a proper family now," she said simply.

Ann bit her lip and blinked hard. "Bless yer," was all she could manage, and at that moment, James returned holding Mary Ann's book aloft.

"I 'ope yer like it."

"Let me see. Shall I read it out?" she asked, knowing that they would not be able to do so.

They both nodded.

"On this day, the Thirtieth of May in the year of our Lord, eighteen-hundred-and-fifty-eight, Mary Ann Knight spinster of this Parish, was joined in Holy matrimony to James Newland, bachelor, at St Mary's church, Selborne. In the sight of Our Lord Jesus Christ.

Also remembered on this day, Mr William Butler and Mrs Butler both deceased, much loved grandparents of the bride and late of this parish.

Signed: Frederick A Parsons. Incumbent."

Mary Ann sat open-mouthed and stared at the page and then she said softly. "It's perfect. Oh, thank you James. I shall treasure this always."

Ann ran quickly from the room, but not before James saw the tears in her eyes.

When the last of the family had left and the remaining neighbours had staggered off home, the two couples sat around the tiny kitchen reminiscing about the day.

"Well, son, yer a married man now." John winked. "This is when all yer troubles start."

"I were surprised at the vicar," said Ann. "'E used to be a bit of a tarter, but 'e seemed to enjoy t'day as much as anyone."

"Yeh, 'e were alright, weren't 'e?" James looked at Mary Ann, his chest almost visibly swelling with pride. "'E did a lovely bit o' writin' in my wife's book."

They all laughed as he uttered the unaccustomed word.

"We'll 'ave to go next door tomorrer an' see what needs doin'," John said tapping out his pipe. "I'll get the key off the manager in the mornin'. That were nice o' Mr Wright..."

But his words were cut off by a sudden loud knock at the door.

"Who on earth..." He opened the door to find a man standing on the doorstep with a large brown paper parcel in his hands.

"This is for Miss Knight ... as was." He handed the package to John, then said 'Goodnight' and was gone.

Mary Ann stared at the parcel. "Who's it from?"

"Best open it an' see," Ann said, as they all gathered around.

John placed it on the table, and with trembling fingers Mary Ann untied the string and peeled back the paper. There were gasps as the wrapping came away to reveal a large clock in a beautiful carved oak case.

Then she picked up the card which had fallen onto the table and read the inscription. For several moments she stood motionless.

"Well?" James asked.

"It's from my grandfather Knight," she said quietly. "He heard that I was getting married and thought that I might like this." And putting the card down, she burst into tears.

"After all this time," Ann said. "Why, after all this time?"

Chapter Eighteen

The old man puffed on his pipe and stared into the fire which burned a fierce red in the black-leaded grate. Outside, the nearby church clock struck three, the sound echoing sharply on the cold air. The sky lowered with green-grey clouds which threatened snow and he hoped that his grandchildren would be home before it started.

He smiled to himself; what a squeeze it was when they were all here. There wasn't really room for him and his wife as well as their son, daughter-in-law and their seven children. Still, they managed, and he liked it here in Bentley. He had never thought to see the day when he would leave Selborne, but sometimes these things happened and Fred and Carrie had offered them a home when they needed it, and they were grateful.

He looked across to where his wife sat sewing on the other side of the fireplace. Her hair was grey now and her blue eyes faded a little, but to him she was still as beautiful as the day they married.

Where had they gone, all those years? What was it now ... almost forty-three he reckoned, and twenty of those had been spent here at Church Cottage.

She caught him looking at her. "You alright dear?" she asked, smiling. "You look tired. Too much gardening yesterday, no doubt." She returned her attention to the sewing. It was a never ending chore in this household, but she never complained—it helped pass the time, as well as keeping the children's clothes looking decent.

"Children'll be in from school soon. Is Carrie due back with the little'uns?"

"Yes, I'll get the kettle on. They'll all need hot drinks, it's bitter out there." Mary Ann rose from her seat, filled the large black kettle and set in on top of the range.

"I 'ope she's wrapped Eva up properly—that babe feels the cold," James said.

"You know Carrie's careful where her young 'uns are concerned —talking of which, she thinks that there may be another on the way."

"Tch, I know it ain't none of our business, but really..." He let out a loud sigh. "There'll be nothin' for it but to move, the rate they're goin' on."

She smiled at him knowingly. "If things had been different, we would probably have ended up with just as many."

His eyes clouded as painful memories returned. He nodded. "Aye, that's true, an' our Fred does work 'ard to keep em all."

They sat in silence for a while, both deep in thought. Mary Ann pulled off more cotton from the reel and threaded her needle again. "Carrie's been a good daughter-in-law too."

Her voice made James jump, and he realised he must have been dozing.

"She didn't hesitate to move in here and help us in our old age," she continued, "not that I feel old—if it weren't for this darned chest of mine…"

He sat watching her for a while as she plied the needle in and out along the hem, until the movement made his eyelids droop again. Perhaps just a few minutes—the children would soon wake him up.

In the silence, the ticking of the clock on the mantelpiece reminded him, as it always did, of their wedding day. What a day that had been, the pair of them brim full of happiness—but happiness that was not destined to last. The wonderful glow in which he'd found himself had dimmed four weeks later when Mary Ann had given birth to their son. A tiny, sickly baby who barely had the strength to cry, but who clung precariously to life for nine weeks. In that time Mary Ann had refused to believe that he would not survive, even when the vicar called at the cottage to baptise him, to save the poor little mite the journey to the church.

James blamed himself. He knew that if Mary Ann had had enough to eat whilst carrying the baby, the child would have been stronger. He should have made more of an effort to get food, but he knew only when it was too late, and when alone he'd shed hot, angry tears of remorse.

They had called the baby James; it was what Mary Ann wanted…

"Cup of tea, dear?" His wife's voice came from afar. She always made tea in times of crisis.

"Thanks," he mumbled, and then opened his eyes and realised that he had been dreaming again. He dreamed a lot nowadays, it was all there seemed to be to do. He had never thought about getting old, not until a couple of years ago when he had been unwell for several months. When the doctor had said that it was his age, he had exploded angrily. What does that fool know, he had thought.

He still had his garden and grew enough vegetables to feed the family—with Fred's help now and again, he conceded. There was not much to be done yet this year, with the winter holding its grip, but once the weather picked up a bit there would be all the spring and summer vegetables to sow.

"Hello, granddad!" The voice was loud in his ear and he opened his eyes to see to see seven-year-old Joseph leaning on the arm of his chair. "Granny says not to let your tea get cold." The child regarded him with serious grey eyes.

"Thank you Joe, good day at school?"

"Yes, thank you. Shall I write you something on my blackboard later?"

He smiled. "That would be nice, I'd like that." The child skipped off to play and James reflected on what a thoughtful boy he was. Quieter and more caring than the others too, I wonder who he takes after? Not his father for sure, Fred was a strong and dependable man with little time for sentiment, as were his sons Frederick, William and Thomas. Nice boys, but rough around the edges, as Mary Ann had put it.

The little girls were all delightful. Florence, who at fourteen had gone out to work in service was more outgoing, but little Rosalie and baby Eva were very quiet and well behaved.

And then there had been Owen. He had been born five years ago, and just like James and Mary Ann, their Fred and Carrie had had to suffer the heartbreak of losing a child. It had been so sudden and unexpected, and it had taken the family a long time to come to terms with it. He had been such a beautiful child, and the loss had shaken his churchgoing parents' faith to the very core. The only way they could cope was by thanking God for the nine months that he had been with them.

James awoke with tears in his eyes. What a sentimental old fool I'm getting, he told himself.

"You alright, dad?" It was his daughter-in-law.

"Oh, it's you Carrie. I didn't hear you come in. I'm fine."

"Dinner's nearly ready, I'll dish up in about five minutes."

He realised now that there was a tantalising smell of meat pie coming from the kitchen. "Right, I must 'ave nodded off for longer than I thought. Are the children all home?"

Carrie gave him a strange look. "Yes, why?"

"I just thought it was time they were in, that's all."

She shrugged her shoulders and shot Mary Ann a questioning glance before hurrying back to the kitchen.

James thought back to the pies his ma had made. His pa always said they were the best in Hampshire, and to tell the truth they were. He had been alright though, because ma had taught Mary Ann how to make them in the same way.

A vivid picture came to his mind of the family at Selborne where, in that tiny kitchen, they all squeezed around the scrubbed wooden table, with pa sat at the head.

He remembered the shock of his father's death. He and Mary Ann had been living in the cottage next door and early one morning his mother had rushed in to tell them he had gone. So sudden, and he had always felt remorse for not having said goodbye.

Someone touched his arm. "Come along dad, your dinner's on the table."

Struggling to open his eyes again, he found Fred at his side. "Oh dear, I am a sleepy-'ead today. Right, I'm comin'."

He joined the rest of the family and Mary Ann studied his face with concern. "You'd better have an early night dear, you look all in."

"I'm alright, it's old age creepin' on, that's all," he laughed.

Fred raised his eyebrows. "You're only sixty-eight dad, that's no age nowadays. Look at the Queen, she was eighty-two when she died t'other week."

"Ah well, if I'd 'ad as good a life as she's 'ad, I'd probably see eighty-odd an' all," he said making them all laugh by pulling a funny face. They fell silent for a moment none the less. "We'll miss 'er though, God bless 'er Majesty." James held up an imaginary glass.

They ate their meal in silence and once the two women had cleared the table and gone into the kitchen to wash the dishes, James settled down in his chair beside the fire once more.

Soon the feeling of warmth and comfort, and the ticking of the clock, made him doze again in spite of the voices of the children who sat round the table doing their sums before bed.

He wished once more that he had learnt to read, write and do a few simple sums. He felt at a disadvantage when his grandchildren asked questions. His parents had never worried about it, nor he guessed, their parents before them, but it was a changing world they lived in—a world which he felt sure his father would not have liked.

He thought of the day that the railway had come to Alton. My, what a commotion that had caused, with the whole village turning out to get their very first sight of a train! He remembered vividly running across a vast field with his son Fred at his side, then only about five years old. It was quite a distance from the village, but most had come on foot and the excitement mounted as they gathered beside the track where metal rails had been put down to carry the thing.

His father had caught up with them and stood trying to get his breath back when the first puffs of smoke appeared in the distance. The children jumped up and down and the adults craned their necks to get a first glimpse of ... they knew not what.

Suddenly, round a bend in the track, roared a monster. He remembered being scared witless as the ground shook beneath his feet, and deafened by the noise as it came nearer.

Many ran away from the trackside, afraid that it would topple over on top of them, and several screamed in fear as the huge engine raced past, its huge metal wheels holding the tracks as though by magic. The carriages clattered and clanked behind it, and those watching were amazed to see the people sitting inside waving at them excitedly.

The choking, acrid smoke billowed across the countryside, almost blotting out the sun, and the crowd put shirt-tails or aprons over their faces to breathe.

James' concern for his son was wasted as Frederick danced around with the other children, delighting in this new phenomenon, but his father stood ashen-faced, hand on heart and shaking his head. And as the train rattled away towards Alton station and the crowd made its way slowly back to Selborne, a deadly hush hung over all. James saw his mother standing at the edge of the field with a few of the other women, and she hurried forward to meet her husband.

"Are yer alright, John? My God that was terrifyin', yer'll never get me on one o' those things, never." James remembered pulling her leg later, when she started using the train regularly to visit Bentley.

His father never did get to like what he called 'all this modern rubbish,' and from then until he died four years later he never ventured out of the village again.

Poor pa, he'd have a few shocks if he were here now, what with horses being replaced by engines fitted to carriages—and some men were even working on a machine which would fly. I ask you, man flying! If we were meant to fly, God would have given us wings. No pa wouldn't have liked it at all...

"James?" He heard Mary Ann calling.

"Yes dear."

"Are you coming to bed? It's getting late," she said. "Mind you, you've been asleep all evening, I can't see you wanting much more." But she was smiling as he eased himself stiffly from the armchair.

"It's this chair they got me, it's too comfy. I drop off every time I sit down. We didn't 'ave chairs like this back 'ome, all big and soft."

They undressed and climbed into the big old bed which had seen them through all the years. It had been almost impossible to get it into the small bedroom—taken three men two days to do, and then only by dismantling and rebuilding it.

James lay on his back, hands behind his head.

"You look thoughtful, dear," said Mary Ann.

"I was thinkin' earlier, that pa wouldn't 'ave liked livin' now. 'E thought machines was evil, an' there's some right strange things goin' on now. Fred tells me yer can talk to people in London on a thing with wires—now that sounds daft, but 'e assures me it's true. 'An' look at these camera things, they're not right—makin' images of people." He shuddered.

Mary Ann shook her head. James had been dead set against having photographs taken since Owen's death. And then losing Tom had made it even worse. She had given up trying to convince him that their deaths had nothing to do with having their pictures taken.

He surprised her by asking suddenly, "Would yer do it all again? Get wed I mean, in spite of all the sadness an' the strugglin'."

She reached across and touched his face gently with her hand. "Of course I would," she said softly. "I've never regretted a single moment of the years I've spent with you. Why do you ask?"

He shrugged. "Just seems like we've 'ad it tough, that's all. Losin' one son were bad enough, but to lose another, an' 'im a father 'imself, seems cruel. An' then George goin' off to Tasmania... Yer've never complained, but yer must 'ave felt like givin' up sometimes."

"I've felt really sad at times dear, but never once did I wish I'd never married you. We've come through it all together, haven't we?"

He nodded and smiled. "That's all a man can ask for." He leaned forward to kiss her warm cheek. "Thank you dear."

She gave him one of her dazzling smiles. "I don't need thanking. I wouldn't have had it any other way. Now, shall I blow out the candle? Then I can cuddle up to your back, it's bitterly cold tonight."

"Goodnight then." James sighed in contentment.

"Night-night, dear."

He settled himself into the familiar mattress, pulled the covers up under his chin and enjoyed the feel of his wife's warm body nestled against his. Behind closed eyelids he kept the picture of her smiling face. To him, she would always be the lovely young girl with glossy, chestnut hair and laughing blue eyes, and he let himself drift off to sleep with that image in his mind.

Pictures from their life together drifted in and out of his dreams; Mary Ann with Frederick and George at pa's funeral, then a year later with Thomas on her knee. She had always been a good mother and the boys had all adored her as he had his mother.

With a stab of pain, he remembered his mother's betrayal. Not long after pa had died she announced that she was getting married again. The shock rippled through the family. Why?

She had all kinds of reasons, but James never wanted to believe any of them and they were estranged for the rest of her life. He had cried silent but angry tears every night at the time, and awoke now to find his pillow wet again. Why, after all these years, was he crying...

He turned over. Mary Ann was fast asleep. Closing his eyes again, he drifted off to remember happier days, just before George decided to emigrate.

He had surprised them when he said he was going abroad to find work, and James had hated the idea but, as usual, Mary Ann gave her support. By that time they lived in Bentley, and George said that he was going with one of his friends to Australia. Ellen was living there he knew, and he hoped that perhaps they might meet, not realising just how vast a country it was; and in the end George and his friend had ended up in Tasmania.

Soon the two men had settled and found work, then they sent for their young ladies to join them, and the next thing they knew they were married with children. George wrote long, newsy letters and Mary Ann used to look forward to reading them out loud. Life sounded marvellous there, and he sometimes wondered if they should have done the same thing when they were young.

His wife had been the strong one through all the years, especially when Thomas had died. Another shock, one of so many, made worse by the fact that it was only a few months after baby Owen had died. James thought that he would never get over the loss—and although he had come to terms with the deaths, he still blamed it on the camera, however illogical he knew it to be.

It had all started when they decided to send George and his wife Annie some photographs of the family. James thought it a strange idea and didn't want to do it, but Carrie arranged it all and they travelled by train to Aldershot one day to have them done.

The pictures had been joyfully received in Tasmania, but James' worst fears had become reality when both Owen and Thomas had died within the year.

He had felt the advancing years keenly then, and he could not have carried on if it had not been for Mary Ann. In the privacy of their room she would hold him in her arms like a child and soothe away some of the pain.

He woke again, found he was drenched in sweat and threw the covers back, letting in a blast of cold air. He shivered and pulled them back again—he didn't want Mary Ann to get chilled.

The window showed as a pale square and he realised that it must have snowed.

Snow... He drifted off to sleep again, remembering the day they should have been married. Then the day they had finally made it—that had been wonderful—but before he could capture it, the dream moved on and became confused. Where had he been when ma died, Bentley or Selborne? Then there was his friend Tom grooming Solomon—he had been really pleased when Mary Ann had agreed to name one of their sons after him, but now ... they were both gone.

He was walking along the hanger with his sons and they clamoured for his attention. Bees buzzed from flower to flower, their droning loud in his ears. It changed to a roar as a huge black monster rushed by belching smoke—now he was on the train with Mary Ann and they were going to Winchester. She wanted to show him the Cathedral, but he had teased her that it would never compare with their own secret one under the beech tree. She had giggled and the other occupants of the compartment had glared their disapproval.

The mighty beech was still there, he had seen it—was it last year?—when they had visited William and his wife Mary. Perhaps it was longer ago...

Now there was Mrs Butler, flapping her apron at Mr Butler to shoo him back out into the garden to remove his muddy boots.

William and Harriet in the kitchen at Selborne, excitedly telling the family that the vicar had agreed to bury father under the Yew tree.

Sound reached his ears, echoing across the years. "James, are you alright dear?"

His eyelids refused to open. He tried to speak, but his lips would not move.

Just let me be, I'm tired.

Another voice. Fred, what did he want? "Dad, are you alright, can you hear me?" James moved a hand and felt the soft material of the eiderdown. Gradually, some strength seeped back into his body and he slowly opened his eyes to see the worried faces of Mary Ann, Fred and Carrie as they stood beside the bed.

"What's the matter?" he managed to say, but his voice sounded strange to his own ears.

"We were worried about you dad," Carrie said. "Mum couldn't wake you at first." She smiled at him. "Do you feel sick, or have you got a pain anywhere?"

He tried to say that he felt fine, but somehow the words would not form. He tried to move his legs, but something was holding them down. All he could do was stare at them and hope they understood.

"I'll send for the doctor." Carrie was always the practical one and hurried from the room.

A thought came to James and he managed one word. "Eva."

Mary Ann smiled widely and put one of her hands over his. "Well dear if you can remember the baby's birthday, you must be alright." Then to Fred she said, "Shall I fetch her?"

Fred nodded and Mary Ann left the room to return a few moment later with Eva.

"Here we are, here's the birthday girl." The toddler was put down on the bed, where she laughed and gurgled and tried to crawl over him.

He willed his arm to move towards her so that he could take the tiny hand in his. He tried to smile and speak to her, but all that happened was a lop-sided twitch. The worried look that passed between his wife and son went unnoticed. He was feeling so tired again.

Someone lifted his arm and placed in under the bedclothes and he forced one eye open a crack to see where Mary Ann was, but she seemed to have left the room.

The effort was too much so he closed it again. Perhaps she had gone to get him a cup of tea, she always made tea in…

His mind drifted again. How lucky he had been to have such a loving family. Where are you Mary Ann? I want you here. What's that noise?

Oh, it's only the wind outside. March winds and April showers, bring forth…

Someone was holding his hand.

The wind was getting worse, rattling the window frame. It rushed and roared until it filled his ears and his head with noise.

Suddenly it stopped. The silence was absolute. And then gradually a great peace washed over him.

Ah yes, it had always been like that here in the garden. His favourite place in the evening.

And it was such was a beautiful evening, with the sun dipping down behind the hanger to cast long shadows across the fields, and overhead the sky was palest blue flushed with rose pink.

It was utterly silent, not even a bird sang. He turned and looked round, and to his amazement, there standing outside the cottage, its brickwork turned to crimson by the setting sun, stood his parents.

They both smiled, wonderful, heart-warming smiles, and held out their arms to him.

An explosion of joy filled his whole being and he scrambled down from the log-pile to go and meet them.

Just as the sun extinguished its light.

Echoes of the Riot

At the October 1996 meeting of the Selborne Association, publisher John Owen Smith brought along three descendants of men convicted for the Selborne Workhouse Riot of 1830, to speak about how the families had fared after their breadwinners had been imprisoned or transported. This transcript tells some of what Jean Newland had to say about her Selborne ancestors:—

The first question most people ask me on hearing of my great-great-grandfather's involvement with the Selborne riots is, "Why wasn't he transported along with all the other participants?" A good question. For if, in fact, John Newland had really been the leader and organiser of the mob he would surely have suffered the same fate instead of getting off with a six-month prison sentence.

The answer, of course, is that he was not the leader—not in the accepted sense of the word—but because he had a horn or bugle, most likely kept from his military service, he was persuaded to walk in front of the mob. It must have made the jeering, noisy throng look pretty impressive.

I am sure he felt it the right thing to do at the time, because although he was a hard-working man, he had a large family to keep on very little money. In fact, the Newland family were paupers, most likely supplementing their living on hand-outs. I try to imagine what it must have been like for him after the fuss had all died down. With the other rioters sentenced and transported, how must he have felt then? I have to assume he kept rather quiet about it, and I'll tell you why.

In 1976 a letter appeared in the *Farnham Herald* from a lady living in Tasmania asking if there were any of the Newland family still living in the area. My father wrote to her and received an answer almost by return. It turned out that she was a cousin of his. Her father, my father's uncle George, had emigrated to Tasmania in 1898, settled well and had a family. Now they wanted to know the family history. Had great uncle George dropped a few hints I wonder?

My father had been born and brought up in Bentley and so it seemed the obvious place to start until an aunt told us that she thought the family had originally come from Selborne. Now, to be honest, I had only the vaguest idea where Selborne was, in spite of the fact that we had lived in Blackmoor when I was a child.

My parents, sister and I came to Selborne one day hoping the vicar would have the parish records to hand, but no such luck—they were by this time all at the Hampshire Record Office at Winchester. While we were in the village, though, we decided to visit the museum in the *Wakes* and found a reference to a John Newland, 'The Trumpeter,' allegedly the leader of the Selborne riots. Could this man be one of our ancestors, we wondered?

My father was cautious, but a visit to the Record Office confirmed the line from John Newland through his son James to his son Frederick, my father's father. Now we knew the connection, but nothing more. And that was how it stayed for a while.

My father died two years later, my mother's health declined, and sadly the correspondence with Tasmania petered out. Nothing more happened until 1993, when over lunch one day some colleagues and I were discussing our family backgrounds. Of course I proudly mentioned my link to Selborne and then, only a few days later, one of the ladies brought me in a copy of an Alton newspaper which had an article about someone having written a book, and a play, about the Selborne riots.

Well, this sounded interesting so I rang and booked a couple of seats for the play, *This Bloody Crew*. What a revelation! The myth of 'The Trumpeter' was exposed, but the story was fascinating nonetheless. And it was a strange feeling seeing your ancestors playing out events before your eyes, I can tell you.

Jean Newland

The myth that the 'Trumpeter' was leader of the riot had been based largely on interviews which W H Hudson recorded with two daughters of John Newland early in the 20th century, and published in his book 'Hampshire Days.' In fact these daughters, Eliza and Harriet, had not been born at the time of the riot, and were passing on to him a family legend which appears to have grown with the telling!

John Owen Smith

Books of local interest by the same publisher

***One Monday in November**—the story of the Selborne and Headley Workhouse Riots of 1830*

During the 'Swing' riots of 1830, according to the famed historians J.L. & Barbara Hammond, "the most interesting event in the Hampshire rising was the destruction of the workhouses at Selborne and Headley." If these riots had succeeded, "the day when the Headley workhouse was thrown down would be remembered ... as the day of the taking of the Bastille." Here a local historian traces the dramatic events of two days of rioting and its aftermath in the villages and beyond.

From the Preface to **One Monday in November**:

John Owen Smith's book is a real contribution to our history. It tells the story of a few tragic days in East Hampshire in 1830, when hungry men, bewildered by falling wages and rising prices, blundered into mob action ....

I am particularly happy to have the chance to introduce the book to the public. A few years ago I researched and wrote a brief account of the riots, so I am probably one of the few people who can appreciate fully how hard Mr Smith must have worked, how thorough and widespread his investigations have been, unearthing ten times more information than I found. He gives us the economic and social background and then recounts the facts, with clarity, humour and impartiality. His sympathies are clear, but he has not made all his rich men villains or all his poor men saints; he has told it "as it happened". Selborne, Headley and Liphook are much in his debt.

L.C.Giles
Vice-Chairman, Bramshott and Liphook Preservation Society

ISBN 1-873855-09-5 May 1993 Paperback, A4 landscape, 40pp, illustrations plus maps.

***RIOT!** or **This Bloody Crew**—an historical drama*

The stage script of the Workhouse Riots story, performed as a community play in October 1993. Includes historical notes.
ISBN 1-873855-01-X November 1993 Paperback, A4 landscape, 36pp, illustrations plus maps.

(Also available on audio cassette as adapted for radio)

A Balance of Trust—*The foundation of The National Trust
and 50 years of history in & around Haslemere, 1855-1905*

Haslemere was, quite literally, on the road to nowhere until the railway arrived in 1859 and opened up the area as a commuter belt. Ready access to and from London then put pressure on the surrounding common land, giving in-comers incentives to buy and to build. In short, the area was earmarked for invasion.

One such commuter was Sir Robert Hunter, legal adviser to the Post Office, whose vision of the need to secure and protect land of natural beauty for the nation created The National Trust.

From his base in Haslemere we are introduced to events and characters of national significance. Famed for its healthy air, the area soon became the haunt of writers, artists, politicians and scientists of repute. People such as Alfred Lord Tennyson, Helen Allingham and Sir Arthur Conan Doyle were all active in the neighbourhood, and we follow their contribution to the debates of the time. Flora Thompson was there too.

Illustrated throughout with many photographs of the period, it will appeal to those interested in the National Trust, the postal service, great literary characters, 'Green' issues, and the fate of threatened open spaces such as Hindhead Common today.
*ISBN 1-873855-12-5 Sep 1995 Paperback, A4 landscape,
60pp, period illustrations plus maps.*

Some Ancient Churches in North East Hampshire
—an illustrated collection of notes

Twelve fascinating churches in the north east corner of Hampshire are described. A map on the back cover guides you through the picturesque lanes of the area, and 33 photographs give both exterior and interior views of each church. Villages include Bentley ("The Village" of TV & Radio), Selborne of Gilbert White fame, East Worldham with the body of Chaucer's wife, Binsted where Montgomery of Alamein lies, and Bramshott, the final resting place for so many Canadian servicemen of the First World War. A short glossary is included for those unfamiliar with some of the architectural terms used. Suitable size for the pocket.
*ISBN 1-873855-11-7 April 1995 Paperback, A5 portrait,
28pp, illustrations plus map.*

Books of local interest by the same publisher (contd)

All Tanked Up—*the Canadians in Headley during World War II*

A story of the benign 'invasion' of a Hampshire village by Canadian tank regiments over a period of four years, told from the point of view of both Villagers and Canadians. Includes technical details of tanks, and full Order of Battle for Canadian Regiments in 1945, as well as many personal reminiscences.

ISBN 1-873855-00-1 May 1994 Paperback, A4 landscape, 48pp, illustrations plus maps.

On the Trail of Flora Thompson—*beyond Candleford Green*

The author has turned detective. In this book, he discovers the true identities behind the pseudonyms which Flora Thompson employed within her writing to hide the identity of the people and places she encountered 'beyond Candleford Green.'

Sir Arthur Conan Doyle and George Bernard Shaw were two among many eminent people who were regular customers in her post office at Grayshott—unaware that the shy young lady sending their telegrams would one day rank alongside themselves on literary shelves.

But the lesser-known characters also lend their own interest to the story. Who was 'Mr Foreshaw,' the retired big-game hunter with whom she had tea on Sunday afternoons? And 'Richard Brownlow,' the young man who met her often, then told her he 'could never marry her'? And 'Bob Pikesley' who taught her how to keep dry in a rainstorm? And the bright-eyed 'Alma Stedman' who kept Flora from 'brooding'?

And who was the unfortunate 'Mr Hertford,' her employer at Grayshott, who eventually stabbed his wife to death shortly after Flora left the village?

These and other riddles are answered. There is also a 'lost' chapter of Flora's own work published here for the first time, and the opportunity to follow literally in Flora's footsteps by taking the suggested 'trails' through the Hampshire countryside she came to love so well.

ISBN 1-873855-24-9 October 1997 Paperback, 144pp, illustrations plus maps.

John Owen Smith, publisher:—
Tel/Fax: (01428) 712892
E-mail: wordsmith@headley1.demon.co.uk
Web Site: www.headley1.demon.co.uk/